Finding the
MAGNIFICENT
In Lower Mundane

Extraordinary Stories About an Ordinary Place

BOB STROMBERG

FINDING THE MAGNIFICENT IN LOWER MUNDANE
Copyright © 1994, 2004 by Bob Stromberg

Library of Congress Cataloging-in-Publication Data
   Stromberg, Bob, 1952-
      Finding the magnificent in Lower Mundane : extraordinary
   stories about an ordinary place / by Bob Stromberg.
         p.cm.
     ISBN 1-894928-48-2
     1. City and town life—United States—Fiction. 2. Humorous
stories, American. I. Title.
    PS3569.T6973F56 1994, 2004   94-25359
    813'.54—dc20   .   CIP

Unless otherwise noted, all Scripture references are taken form the Holy Bible: New International Version (North American Edition), copyright © 1973, 1978, 1984 by the International Bible Society. Used by permission of Zondervan Bible Publishers.

Edited by Janet Kobobel and Lori Walburg
Cover design by Nikki Braun
Interior design by Larissa Bartos

Word Alive Press Edition

WORD ALIVE PRESS

131 Cordite Road
Winnipeg, Manitoba, Canada
R3W 1S1 www.wordalive.ca

94 95 96 97 98 99 / DH / 10 9 8 7 6 5 4 3 2 1

To Judy, Nate, and Lars
I love you

Contents

Acknowledgements

To Forest Dahl, Diane Harvey, Peter Hawkinson, Bill Howarth, and Bill Stenberg. Thank you for sharing your threads of experience and truth with me. I enjoyed them when they happened and even more while weaving them into my fiction. The tapestry would never have been the same without you.

To my wife, Judy, and my sons, Nate and Lars, who lived so many of these stories the first time and then had to live them again while I wrote these pages. Thank you for your love, your constant encouragement, and your many helpful suggestions. Thank you too, Judy, for the laptop, which I told you I didn't really need. What a wonderful gift.

To my editors, John Sloan and Janet Kobebel. John, thanks for your encouragement in the crucial early going. Thanks too for your wisdom in bringing Janet on board. Janet, you know I speak the truth when I say that you're not only the *best* editor I've ever had, but you're also the *only* one. Thanks for your excellent work. You've made it fun. Also to Lori Walburg, thanks for offering your jar of final editorial polish. It brought out the grain and helped the light reflect more brightly on my stories.

To my friend Scott Bolinder, who first said, "That sounds like a great idea." Thank you for encouraging me to write.

To the people of Port Allegany, Pennsylvania, and Blandford, Massachusetts, two of the most beautiful small towns in America. Thank you for the years you allowed me to be one of you.

And to you, the reader, wherever you live. I hope this book brings you much joy. Isn't God magnificent?

CHAPTER 1

Finding the MAGNIFICENT in Lower Mundane

I've lived many places in my life. I've lived in big cities and tiny burghs. I've lived on farms and in apartment buildings. I've lived beneath a canopy of jungle and in the shade of a freeway. Most always I've been content. However, having recently moved to Lower Mundane, I think I can now say I'm finally home.

The Chamber of Commerce has erected a sign on the edge of town that reads, "Welcome to Lower Mundane, home to some of the world's finest people!"

Last week some kids spray painted out the word "finest." The change rendered the slogan less controversial and perhaps more accurate.

Usually folks get here via Route 6, but it's almost as fast and twice as beautiful to take Old Country Road H from the airport, over the bridge, and to the fork in the road. From there you can take your pick. Either way, you'll end up here. If you're like most folks, either way you go, you'll wonder if you should have taken the other way.

The town was incorporated only fifty years ago by Swedish and Italian immigrants. Apparently these groups of people were living here seventy-five years earlier but couldn't communicate well enough or cooperate long enough to register the town with the state.

Even today the old folks fall pretty much into classes of heritage and religion. Those with the Catholic names such as Rosetti, Rialti, and Berdino live on the hillside in rather large homes, while the Protestant Pearsons, Lindalls, and Sandells reside nearer the river in equally tidy though somewhat smaller homes.

This has always been a point of contention for the Swedes, who were flooded out periodically before the state put up the new levee in the late 1950's. After all these years, Emil Roseen still enjoys complaining to his old nemesis Tom Gucci: "Don't talk to me about how much money I've put into my boat. If I lived on your street up there in Beverly Hills, I wouldn't need one."

The two old guys are both in their eighties, and even though no one would suggest it to them, they do seem to enjoy one another.

In recent years the ethnic lines have softened some, as many new people have moved to Lower Mundane, nearly doubling its population. None of the old folks ever expected this to happen.

"Who would intentionally move here?" they wondered. "And why would we ever want 'em?"

Well, as it turned out, quite a few of us wanted to move here. Because we are so far from the metro area, it seemed unlikely the town would ever become a bedroom community. But when the new airport went in between Lower Mundane and the city, everything changed. Add to that the excellent property values, better than average schools, and quite a lovely natural setting on the river, and Lower Mundane began to look rather attractive. Attractive but for its name.

Just last month the wound festered again when Rosellen Powell, the recently installed Christian education director at Grace Megatabernacle, wrote a letter to the editor of the *Reporter Argus* advocating, for the umpteenth time, that we change Lower Mundane's name to something else.

Powell's letter, entitled, "Let Me Tell You What's in a Name," was the first, however, to argue for a change on purely spiritual grounds.

"Shortly after moving to Wycoff, Michigan, in 1988," Powell writes, "I learned my daughter's high school mascot was a blue demon. I pointed out the name's inappropriateness, and the school board, comprised of reasonable, intelligent, and spiritually sensitive people, agreed. The name was changed to the Wycoff Wildcats."

I later discovered that Powell neglected to mention her threat to remove her daughter, Penny, from girl's varsity basketball. This is Pistol Penny, who appeared in the back of *Sports Illustrated* as a junior in high school. Pistol Penny Powell, the Princess of Purdue, who last year led the

Boilermakers to the "final sixteen." Pistol Penny, whose smiling face appears on the signs outside of town greeting visitors with a "Welcome to Wycoff, 1990 Girls' Basketball State Champs."

Powell continued her argument, "I didn't want my children being called Blue Demons, and I don't want my town called Mundane. We might as well say we are from East Carnality or Upper Worldliness, for that is exactly what the word 'mundane' means. Add to that the prefix 'lower,' and we're even worse off. Why don't we just come out and name our town Hell!"

Well, for weeks the letters flowed off the editorial page right into the hospital discharges and obituaries. One letter came from a high school dropout, Ted Mumford. Ted, who currently works at the tannery in Chastain, didn't understand that Rosellen was being sarcastic. He said he agreed with her, and he cast his vote to change the name to Hell.

Others wrote to say they disagreed with Rosellen's definition of "mundane." Several folks, including Winifred Rossi, who owns half the town, said their dictionaries also defined "mundane" as synonymous with "regular", "ordinary," and better yet, "practical."

At the editor's encouragement, many people sent in possible new names for consideration. Springfield was high on the list, the reasoning being ours is one of the few states that doesn't have one. Such thinking caused one writer to respond, "Oh, fine! So we go from Mundane to Inane."

Also Riverview, Riverside, Rivercrest, Riverton, Poplar Bend, and Mundyville were suggested. No one seemed to notice that all of these ideas were far more ordinary and regular than Lower Mundane, which may be the only one in the world.

The last letter came from Emil Roseen, who wrote, "I for one am sick of all this silly talk for changing our name. Our town is what it is, and we are what we are. And frankly, for the most of us, 'mundane' is an appropriate adjective. Whether you define it as worldly or just plain regular, that describes us all quite accurately. So why lie about it?

"Go ahead, Rosellen and all you folks out there at the Megatab, change our town to Buena Vista, but we'll still be living right here in Lower Mundane, and you all know it."

The letters have petered out since then, tempers have cooled, and most people have begun to forget about the issue. But not me.

You see, though I might have tried to express myself a bit more sensitively, I happen to agree with Emil. Wherever I've lived, much of the time has been in lower mundane. My life has always had a carnal, worldly side, and in many respects it has been quite ordinary and regular.

But lately something exciting has begun to happen. I'm discovering that right here, in Lower Mundane, the God of the universe is revealing himself in magnificent ways. Right here in this worldly place, in my carnal heart, through very ordinary happenings, God is doing magnificent things.

Some of these things I've discovered while reflecting on my life in other locales and times. Some of these things I've recognized while living right here in town. All of these revelations have changed the way I look at life.

As you read my recollections and ponderings, may you recognize yourself in Lower Mundane and reflect on God's magnificence in your life, even today.

CHAPTER 2

Old Doc Elder
and
His Miracle Cure

God whispers to us in our pleasures,
speaks in our conscience, but shouts in our pains;
it is his megaphone to rouse a deaf world.

C.S. Lewis, The Problem of Pain

I'd been having some trouble with my feet. At first I didn't think much of it. It felt as though I had a piece of gravel in my shoe, maybe a small blister. But after several months, it began to feel more like a large cinder or a little GI Joe. Eventually when I slipped on a shoe it felt like I was shoving my foot into a box of tacks.

Finally it occurred to me that I might look at the bottom of my foot. That's when I saw the horrible truth.

I suppose it's something I ought not feel embarrassed about. Hey, this kind of thing could happen to anyone, right? Anybody could get 'em. Somehow though, I'd lived for forty some years, and they'd just never happened to me before. I guess it's partly because, as a child, I'd been forced to step on those little antifungal spray machines after my showers in gym class and at the gate to the community pool.

As I looked at the strange, volcanic shapes on my soles, I realized I hadn't sprayed anything on my feet in years.

If I had been a child, my mother would have had me down to Doc Helman's office at the first sign of trouble. He would have prescribed some expensive cream, and in a week or so I'd have been fine. But Doc Helman had been dead for years. I was an adult myself now, and my young family and I hadn't yet found a doctor in our new community of Lower Mundane.

The truth is I didn't particularly care to look for one. It's not that I have anything against doctors. I'm just very displeased with the way the medical profession has changed since I was a kid.

I can explain it like this. When I go into a clothing store to buy a pair of pants, I usually walk out a little while later with the new pants and maybe even more. I don't have to wait for a receptionist, who makes me fill out countless forms and answer personal questions like "How long have you been a 33 x 33? Do you have a family history of short inseams? Any allergies to natural fabrics? Are you currently wearing any other prescription polyesters? Do you have insurance to cover the pants, or will you be paying for them yourself?"

No, when I go to the store for a pair of pants, I don't have to walk down a hallway to some little room and sit on a rolled-out piece of white wrapping paper for twenty minutes, staring at artistic renderings of dungaree dissections while I wait for a salesperson to come and ask me why I came to the store.

Then, after all this time, the person will say, "Yes, I can see that your old pants are in pretty bad shape, and I think you were wise to come in before they get any worse. So on your way out, just stop by the receptionist's desk, pay for this visit, and make an appointment for some time next month. I'm sure we can find you something you'll be comfortable wearing."

When I want to buy a pair of pants, I walk into the store, find what I want, pay for it, and walk out. And that's kind of the way it used to be with Doc Helman. You would walk in with a temperature. You would walk out with a prescription. If you walked in with a cut, you walked out with stitches. When you walked in with the flu, you walked out with a shot. It wasn't an ordeal. But times have changed.

So I asked Pross Worthy, an older gentleman from my church who has lived in Lower Mundane for years, if he could suggest a family clinic where I wouldn't have to go through all the hoopla.

"Listen," he said. "I can do better than that. Why don't you forget the clinic and go to Old Doc Elder? His wife is his only nurse. He has one little waiting area, no computers, no receptionist, and lower overhead 'cause he works out of the back of his house. I've been going to him since my mother was pregnant. He's a man of very few words with sixty years of experience from the old no-nonsense school of medicine. A bit odd perhaps, but believe me, if he can't take care of your feet, nobody can. And he'll cost you maybe half what you'd pay at a clinic."

Well, this sounded good to me, so I called and made an appointment, surprisingly, for that very day.

From the moment I walked into the empty waiting room I felt I had been sent back in time. The couches were covered with old green leather, heavily cracked with age— just like Doc Helman's furniture. In fact, just like Doc Helman. The couches' arms were scratched tubular stainless steel that would have been something to talk about back in '63. It appeared no money had been spent recently on decorating. The wallpaper, the lamp shades, the old Persian rugs, even the collection of children's Golden Books and the faded ring stack toddler toy were all circa 1955. A jar of black licorice jellybeans sat on the end table.

The only items that looked remotely modern were the two Radio Shack minispeakers mounted near the ceiling through which, remarkably, Perry Como sang some old familiar classic that my dad used to whistle. Heavy wooden French doors, covered with lacy curtains, led to the office area. On the wall a sign read "Please have a seat." So I did.

I sat on the shiny stiff leather for no more than a minute when one French door opened. An elderly, gray-haired gentleman in a white lab coat entered the room humming something Glen Miller's band had begun to play. His posture looked painfully poor. His shoulders rounded severely, giving him a caricatured appearance. Undoubtedly this was the result of sixty long years leaning over patients, peering into tiny ear canals. But that was not my immediate impression of the doctor.

It seemed to me he was leaning forward due to the weight of his enormous glasses, which he wore precariously near the end of a long weathered nose. The frames were heavy herringbone, which appeared necessary to support the thickest bottle-bottom lenses I'd ever seen. The only other impression was of great age. I guessed late eighties, maybe early nineties.

I was just about to say, "Hello, I'm Bob Stromberg. I called earlier today about a three o'clock appointment." But I realized he didn't see me. He was walking directly toward me; I could see his dark owlish pupils, magnified through the telescopes he wore on his long sloping nose. He seemed to look me straight in the eye, but I knew he didn't see me.

Just when I thought he might walk right into me, he stopped. Reaching down to grab a handful of jellybeans, he turned and shuffled back into his office, scratching the side of his leg and mumbling something about people who can't be on time for their appointments.

When he closed the French door behind him, I surprised myself by exhaling a long breath I hadn't realized I was holding. Well, that was enough for me. The clinic was beginning to sound like an attractive alternative after all. I stood to leave, but the door swung open again, and this time revealing a tiny, bright-eyed woman, close to seventy perhaps, dressed in white and not quite five feet tall.

"Well, there you are. You must be Bob," she said in a playful, somewhat condescending tone. Then wagging an accusatory finger, she added, "Bob's got some little warties on his feet, doesn't he?"

"Well…ah…yes, I guess he does," I stammered, a little embarrassed by her use of what I guessed to be improper medical terminology. I was sensing that perhaps it would be best at this point to say that I needed to reschedule my appointment—then conveniently forget to show up. But I never had the chance to speak.

"Well, all right, come on in then," she said, suddenly all business. "The doctor's been waiting."

The office consisted of a long oak table, the familiar roll of paper attached to one end; against a wall stood a heavy walnut desk, and in the corner a white metal cabinet with a glass door displayed an assortment of syringes, tiny bottles, and bright blue boxes of gauze bandages.

Old Doc Elder sat in an ancient wooden swivel chair. He was intently bent over his desk with a tube of airplane glue in his right hand. The walnut desk was covered with newspapers on which sailed a partially completed plastic model of a World War I destroyer. Not stopping his work for a second, he indicated the oak table with a sideways nod.

He mumbled a bit menacingly, "Have a seat." And then, almost as if it were a dare, "Do you want to remove your shoes and socks?"

I did as he asked while his wife put on rubber gloves and sterilized shiny things over by the medicine cabinet.

Several moments later, having glued a long piece of artillery to the smokestack on his ship, he shuffled his feet, rolling his chair backward toward my table. Then spinning around, he brought his nose within four inches of the bottom of my left foot. Here he immediately became enthralled with his work. Squinting hard, with his mouth gaping wide, he appraised my problem as a jeweler might a fine gem, all the time mumbling, "Heavenly glory! Will you just look at this!"

After what seemed like a long time, he eased back in his chair. Pulling a white hanky out of his coat pocket to wipe the sweat off his brow, he asked incredulously, "Are you going to try to tell me, son, that you got these right here in the U.S. of A.?"

Before I could answer, before I could ask him if they were really that bad, he called to his wife, "Margarite, look at these feet! Worse than anything I ever saw in the trenches. Come over here, dear, and bring the Polaroid."

"Well, Doc," I said brightly, trying to salvage any remaining dignity, "I was told that if anyone can fix me, you can."

The doctor did not respond. While Margarite flashed away, he stood right up, much straighter than I thought possible, and walked toward the supply cabinet with the determination of a younger man on a mission.

"I heard you were the guy to burn these things off or zap 'em, or whatever it is you do." I chuckled nervously, my skin growing moist.

The voice that responded to me sounded nothing like the uninterested mumble of the old model maker who had greeted me only moments before. No, the voice sounded excited, youthful, like a kid on summer vacation asking his father, "Really, Dad! You mean I get to gut the fish all by myself?"

Old Doc Elder turned to me and, with his face sparkling, nearly shouted, "So, young man, do you want that newfangled zappin' thing, or do you want to be healed?" In his hand he held what looked like a big Exacto knife.

At this point I may be a little fuzzy on some details. I'm not at all certain, for example, how long I remained in the office after this.

I *do* remember his wife though. With her back to me, she grabbed my foot and hoisted it under her right armpit, sort of the way one might shoe a horse.

When Doc Elder said, "Hold it real still now, darlin'," she leaned back on my calf, trapping my ankle between herself and the oak table. That's when I heard him say, "Hang on, Billy, I'm going in!"

I wanted to say, "Just exactly what is it you mean by 'going in'? What about some Novocain? Hey! Don't you have to freeze it or something? *Hold it! Time out!*"

But there wasn't time. As Old Doc Elder, grasping his scalpel like a dagger, plunged into my foot, all I could do was grab the edge of the table and try to stay conscious.

I can't entirely trust my recollection at this point, but it seemed as though the two of them were having fun.

After some timelessness, the surgeon turned around. Holding a small stainless steel bowl in his bloody rubber gloves, he proudly displayed, for my approval, several pieces of foot that he had removed. "That's the three biggest ones," he said, "I think that ought to do it."

This was not exactly good news. I knew about a dozen little ones were still down there, but I couldn't imagine going through this again. Sweating badly, lying back on the table, and trying to regain some composure, I expressed my concern. "Only three! You mean you only got three?"

Old Doc Elder, chuckling, put my mind at ease. "No, no, son. The rest of them are going to go all by themselves, and they're going to go quickly. Your body will just take care of 'em. You see, there's no way your body will let you go through that again."

After a few moments, when I was able to stand by myself, I offered to write him a check. But he said, "Naw, Margarite will send you a bill." And then he walked me to the door with his arm around my shoulder, as though I was some close friend who had stopped over and done him a favor.

I never heard from Margarite, and then later down at the Old Corner Store I learned that Doc Elder had passed on to that great operating room in the sky. That was two years ago, and I've not had a problem with my feet since.

Recently I took my boy Lars to the new clinic to have a wart removed. His doctor froze the foot with some icy spray and then burned the growth with that "newfangled zappin' thing." As he worked, my son listened while I told the doctor about my experience with Old Doc Elder. Several times he had to stop working while he wiped away tears of laughter.

Then I asked, "Tell me, doctor, how did he know the others would go away by themselves?"

"Well, you see," he said, "the wart doesn't belong to your foot. In fact, it doesn't even belong on your body. It's foreign material growing there, and ordinarily the body would expel it all on its own. But for some unknown reason, in the case of warts, the body doesn't recognize that the wart is destructive, alien material. So the body just lets them spread and become worse and worse.

"That's why I'm burning Lars's foot. I'm not burning off the growth. I'm just burning around it. But that means he's going to have some blisters here and experience some pain. When the body sends help to check out the pain, it will notice the warts at the same time and decide to do something about them too.

"A little pain is a magnificent thing when it comes to alerting the body to a problem and initiating the healing process."

What he said made a lot of sense to me. I told him if he ever decides to get out of medicine he can always teach at a seminary.

CHAPTER 3

Adventures of a Mundane Man

I've noticed people here in Lower Mundane don't often comment about the weather. In other parts of the country, weather is the preferred topic of trivial conversation. If you have nothing to say to someone, you can always remark about the weather.

"Wow, it's a hot one today, ain't it!"

"Yeah, it sure is. I sweat clear through my undies just walkin' to the mailbox!"

Go into any convenience store anywhere in America, and someone's talking about the weather. Beautiful day … Looks like rain … Might be some heavy fog … Better bundle up … Watch the icy bridge … Don't forget your sunscreen … Thank God for air conditioning!

People seem the most friendly when they're talking about the weather. Maybe it's simply because we all have weather in common, but I think something deeper is happening here. I think we long for a sense of shared adventure, something we have to brave together, an obstacle that we dare not face alone. And weather has always been a formidable enemy.

It wasn't the mountains that trapped the Donner party, it was the weather. It wasn't the altitude that thwarted so many expeditions a few hundred feet short of the world's great summits, it was the weather.

I remember as a teenager watching in amazement as Neil Armstrong bounded like an arthritic nymph on the surface of the moon. In the foreground I could see the aluminum leg of his ship. He had traveled a quarter million miles through space and descended to the moon's surface in a crude-looking tinfoil vessel with less computer technology than an '87 Volkswagen Jetta.

Yet, for me, the event was anticlimactic. Why? I think it was the lack of weather. Deep down I guess I'd hoped to see him emaciated and scorched, in rags like Robinson Crusoe, or with snow and frost plastered to his frozen face like Sir Edmund Hillary. In my mind, all great explorers have to defeat weather. But the only weather threatening to cut off communication and destroy the moon mission was the snowy reception of my black and white RCA. In the colorless Sea of Tranquility there was no weather. Armstrong, antiseptic and chubby in his marshmallow suit, bantered on and on while awkwardly driving golf balls over the lunar landscape. Certainly the dangers were numerous, but without weather they seemed as colorless as my TV screen.

I think that's why we like to talk about weather. Throughout history it's always been the agent of our most exciting adventures. So we encourage one another.

"If I were you, I wouldn't even mow the lawn today. Way too hot! Better stay inside."

"Yeah, sure you shoveled the whole driveway by yourself last week, but this snow is much wetter. I tell you, this storm is a widow-maker. You better get someone to plow it for you."

Nothing is more normal than to talk about the weather. But in Lower Mundane, people don't do it. They just don't do it! This is particularly odd because, of all places, the weather is remarkable here. Since the town is nestled near the river low on the northwest hillside, very little direct sunlight ever reaches us during the winter months. For this reason and others, probably unknown even to meteorologists, Lower Mundane is typically the coldest spot in the state from November through April. It can be thirty below zero for ten days in a row, but the most you'll hear someone say is, "Little nippy."

During the summer, any hint of a cool breeze whispering down the river elevates about a half-mile upstream and leaves us stifled in heat and humidity. Walk into your local store on these afternoons, and you might hear someone say, "Bit muggy." The person doesn't even expect a response!

I think the attitude among those raised in these parts is, "Hey, you knew the weather was extreme when you moved here. There's no reason to complain. If you don't like it, well, you can always move. Besides, it sure doesn't help to talk about it now, does it?"

Of course these people are made of skin too, so I have to believe they feel the weather just as much as I do. But they won't let on. Not ever.

Last week it snowed forty-three inches in three and a half hours. The storm was not forecast. My pastor, Ryan Care, drives the snowplow, but he was preaching out of town Sunday evening and was unable to get home, so the streets quickly became impassable.

Early Monday morning, in the middle of a luscious sleep, I felt Judy reaching over me to pull back our bedroom curtains.

"Oh, Bob," she said, "look at this!"

Lower Mundane was a fairyland. From our window we could see morning's dazzling display as sunlight sparkled through the river valley. All the town's sharp edges were hidden beneath soft sloping drifts that rose along the side of buildings and hung heavily along the eaves. Three inches of white sat upon the sagging telephone lines. The branches of the maple in our front yard drooped beneath their burden of beauty.

The cold air in our bedroom and the absent digital display on the clock radio confirmed our suspicion that power lines were down. I felt an invigorating nudge of adrenaline. This had the potential to be an adventure!

As we pulled on jeans, woolen socks, and sweaters, we walked through the upstairs inspecting our transformed neighborhood from the vantage point of each window. In my excitement I was tempted to wake our two boys, who still slept soundly beneath their heavy quilts, but there was no rush. There certainly would be no school today, maybe even all week. They had plenty of time to enjoy this new world.

As I opened the last shutter on the bathroom window overlooking the driveway, Judy came up behind me and peered over my shoulder. "We're definitely going to need some milk and juice." She said. "Do you suppose you could get the car out?"

I laughed and pointed toward the driveway below where a huge drift completely hid the garage door. "What do you think?" I asked.

After checking the water pipes and stoking the wood stove, I entered the garage through the kitchen. I retrieved my cross-country skis from their rack, carried them back through the house, and took them out onto the front porch. My wilderness wife stood at the front door to wave me off.

"I'll be home by spring thaw," I said. "Tell the children I love 'em, and keep the double-barrel loaded, just in case you have any more trouble with them grizzlies."

Then I snapped on my skis and, with my backpack and short grocery list, I poled half a mile right down the middle of State Highway 14 toward the center of town. Of course, most everything was closed, but I figured by now Donny Barnes would be doing a brisk business at the Old Corner Store. Since he lives in the apartment directly above he'd have no trouble getting to work. Besides, lots of people were sure to find a way into town to stock up on necessities.

Sure enough, as I skied into the parking lot and over a drift nearly concealing the gasoline pumps, I saw lined against the store window half a dozen cross-country skis, several pairs of snow shoes, and a plastic supply sled emblazoned with a decal of Yukon Snoopy. I entered the store victorious, feeling every bit like Ernest Shackleton reaching the South Pole.

In the store, several old guys stood around the coffee pot, and a few hardy women walked the two aisles, filling their arms with potato chips and toilet paper.

Pulling off my ski mask, I nearly shouted, "Wow, is this *beautiful* or what?"

A stringy-haired, middle-aged lady wearing a pudgy snowmobile suit looked at me. "Yeah, well, whatever," she said.

"Aaah," one of the old guys growled, "this is nothing compared to April '53."

I looked around for support. Everybody else in the store just stared at me blankly, the snow slowly melting from their boots and dripping on the floor.

I shrugged and turned away. Their nonreaction didn't matter. For me this was awesome beauty and adventure. My family and I were stranded in our home with no electricity, no TV, no microwave, no radio, and no lights, and we were going to enjoy every minute of it.

By the time I returned home, the boys were up and already burrowing tunnels out of the garage. Judy had bacon and eggs sizzling on top of the wood stove. We settled in to wait out the storm in cozy comfort.

Having provided for our immediate needs, I felt as if I had not a care in the world. I couldn't make calls or send faxes. I couldn't negotiate contracts or send our promotions. After all, we were marooned—shut off from the rest of the world. By now CNN would be reporting our plight via satellite, maybe even deploying a helicopter for aerial footage. What an adventure!

I headed downstairs to check for frozen pipes. There I discovered in our basement storage one last box of unpacked books. I thought, *This would be a great time to finally get these unpacked and arranged upstairs.*

So I hauled the box up to the family room, sat on the floor, and proceeded to sort. I picked up the first book ... Louis L'Amour's autobiographical *Education of a Wandering Man.* I had always meant to read it. Intrigued, I opened the book.

Louis L'Amour told how he left school at fifteen to roam the world. He hopped freight cars, rode the Southern Pacific rails with the hobos, skinned dead cattle in Texas, survived a two-day solo walk out of Death Valley, and sailed to Singapore while making extra cash along the way as a bare-knuckle prize fighter. In addition to all that, L'Amour read more than one hundred books per year and later published nearly that many of his own.

I put down the book, depressed. I should have felt excited about his adventures. But in comparison, he made my life seem a bit experientially deficient.

To make matters worse, the next book I picked up was *Four Against Everest* by Woodrow Wilson Sayre. I had read this book several years ago. It told of Sayre's journey with three friends to the top of the world's highest mountain. The four men had meager climbing experience, no financial sponsorship, antiquated gear, and little more than extra socks and backpacks. Sayre himself fell repeatedly, once sliding a thousand feet down the North Face, over a cliff. Yet he lived to write a book about it!

Honestly, I hardly ever do that kind of thing. And I have no doubt that Sayre would not have been overly impressed with my trek to the Old Corner Store.

Before I could do my ego any more damage, I quickly stacked the books onto the shelves, willing myself not to look at the titles. I didn't care to compare myself to other great explorers and adventurers. My life would always pale in comparison.

But late in the evening, as we boiled water over the wood stove to warm our evening baths, I sat at the kitchen table in the glow of a kerosene lantern. In my left hand I held a cup of cocoa and in my right a pen. I decided to take stock and see if my life really had lacked those special moments so apparent in others' lives.

I started my notes on a small Post-It note pad, thinking the space would be adequate, but was pleased to find the need to move on to a table napkin. Following are ten memories I discovered. Ten memories that still give me a little thrill.

1. When I was six, I sat on the laundry room floor one cold winter evening and stared into the warm spot between the Maytag and the wall. There, nestled in an old bed sheet, our cat Sparkle licked clean five little blind kittens. And then to my amazement, right before my eyes, came the sixth.

2. When I was nine, I helped my dad pull a thirty-two inch pike into an old wooden rowboat. I held it to the bottom of the boat, my small hands barely crossing the fish's slimy girth, while my dad removed the hook. I realize it's an anachronism, but in my memory I swear I hear the *Jaws* theme song.

3. As a high school junior, in the din of a championship basketball game, I sat on the bench with fourteen seconds remaining and heard my coach shout,

"Strommy!" My knees went weak. We were down by four points with no time-outs and no three-point line, but in the final seconds, thanks to my teammate's defense and my opponent's trip over the foul line, I scored six points in slow motion from some inner world, deep in the corner with 0:01 left on the clock, I launched the last shot from my hip ... nothing but net!

4. During college I memorized the entire tenor line to Mahler's Eighth Symphony and sang it under the direction of Sir George Solti with the Chicago Symphony Orchestra and Chorus. People shouted, "Bravo! Bravo!" I've not often since heard this response. This was exciting for a kid who was really a baritone and couldn't read a lick of music.

5. I lay next to my beautiful young wife on top of a water tower deep in the heart of Africa. Together we gazed for hours at a sky so blazing with constellations that soft shadows danced in the jungle below.

6. One March night I sat in a friend's dog sled on the Alaskan tundra listening to the eerie celestial crackling of the aurora borealis sweeping across the starry sky like colored sheets of electric rain.

7. I witnessed the births of our two sons and their first terrifying flights, gasping, grasping, feet pulled beneath them on an arc through surgical white light and down into their mother's arms. There, through teary eyes, I watched them bob their heavy heads, nuzzling their soft way to a first sweet, warm, homemade meal.

8. On my thirty-fifth birthday, floating high above the Berkshires of Massachusetts, I spit from the gondola of a hot air balloon and watched it fall (the spit, not the

gondola) clear into the forest canopy three quarters of a mile below. Everyone should try this.

9. I performed 475 assembly programs during one school year. I think this experience comes pretty close to sliding a thousand feet down the North Face.

10. I packed my family into a car and followed a moving van headed west, away from all that we had grown to love. Behind in a quaint little village we left friends, family, and a beautiful home with an impossibly low mortgage, a home we had to board up because it had not been sold. Ahead waited a third-floor apartment in the big city and an uncertain future. Why did we leave? Because we thought God wanted us to.

I sat in the lamp's yellow warmth and read the list over and over, each memory capturing a stage in my life. Why did I still feel excited just remembering them, and why, of all the experiences in my life, did these particular ones come to mind?

Then I realized the most important one didn't even make the list. It didn't make the list because it was not particularly exciting at the time. It was just the pensive act of a child in response to hearing the truth.

You see, one day as a young boy, I decided to choose a guide rather than go it alone, figuring if I tried to go it alone, life's adventures would probably kill me. Quite naively, I asked Jesus to be my adventure guide, and he accepted this offer.

I was just a little boy, unaccustomed to research, so I didn't know a whole lot about him. But I thought he was worth the risk. I figured he knew all about the world because he made it, and he seemed to embrace the spirit of adventure. After all, he not only rode the high seas, but he also walked on them. He not only climbed the high mountains, but he also flew off them.

Later I discovered that this was just the beginning of his resumé. Here was a man who lived with primitive tribes, teaching them about God, touching lepers who sought his healing, and facing mobs who wanted to stone him. Ultimately the indigenous peoples nailed him to the limbs of a tree and left him hanging there. But—are you ready for this?—even then he wouldn't give up the adventure. He died, went all the way to hell and back, and still lived to have a book written about it!

L'Amour, Sayre, Armstrong, Shackleton, Hillary—all understood that the adventure reveals the character of the adventurer. If this is indeed true, then this adventurer I have chosen to follow can be none other than the almighty God.

The cocoa-stained napkin is now pressed between the heavy covers of my journal, and the list of adventures grows longer each day. To be sure, if you were to read it quickly, you might think some of them quite mundane, but nothing could be farther from the truth. Each one has the signature of magnificence. Number eleven reads:

I sat by the stove on a snowy night, and wrote by the light of a kerosene lamp.

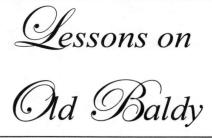

CHAPTER 4

Be still, and know that I am God.

(Psalm 46:10)

Judy struggles with the whole idea of living here. She's a city girl at heart. She loves a great skyline and bright lights. She adores attending the symphony and the ballet. She longs for a large grocery store within the borders of her own state.

For me, living here has not demanded a great adjustment. I don't think it's easier for me because I'm more adaptable than she, but because, compared to where I grew up, Lower Mundane seems cosmopolitan.

My hometown was not in the middle of nowhere, but you could see nowhere clearly from where I lived. When people ask me where I come from, I tell them that I grew up in a little town in north-centralish Pennsylvania.

"Oh really," they respond. "What's it near?"

I tell them it's near south-westernish New York. You see, it's not really near anything. The nearest big city (Buffalo) is about a hundred miles away, but I never knew anyone who had actually been there, and I knew *I* never wanted to go. The only three TV stations we received in my little town were broadcast from Buffalo, so I had watched the local news enough to know I was better off staying right where I was. Every night I'd hear about the killer fires in suburban Cheektowaga or the four-alarm blazes in lower Lackawanna. When, as a junior in high school, I finally *did* drive with my family to the city for the Ice Capades, I was surprised there were any buildings left standing.

I guess you'd say we were a bit isolated in my little town, but we liked it that way. On the radio dial all I could get during the day was WFRM (The Farm and Home Broadcasting Company) from Coudersport. However, on cold, clear winter nights (the kind in which air froze inside my nose), if I tuned my Sears Silvertone very carefully, I might pick up WABC New York, CKLW in Detroit-Windsor, Cousin Brucey at WBZ in Boston, or Dick Biondi at WLS in Chicago.

"Radar weather, eye-eeeee-iiiii-eeeee-iiiii," the weatherman's choir sang in four-part harmony. "Radar weather, eye-eeeee-iiiii-eeeee-iiiii."

"This is Dick Biondi, and it is cold in Chicago. Radar weather has 41 in Des Plaines, 39 on the North Shore and, hey, Chicago, it's a windy 37 in The Loop."

Tucked in my bed, with my blanket up over my ears, I lay in the dark night after night and wondered what a Loop was. I figured it was just more big city stuff I didn't understand, and I didn't think I'd probably ever need to. I liked it just fine right where I was.

No, we didn't have the bright lights, subways, fancy restaurants, or a Loop, but what we had was beautiful. Everywhere one looked it was beautiful.

The rolling Allegheny Mountains, like a long sleeping dog, protected our little town, a suckling pup nosing into her side. Everywhere there were forests and creeks. And, oh, the seasons! Hot green summers. Flaming paint-palette autumns. Crisp deep winters. Ankle-deep muddy, hope-filled springs.

All the little towns around were beautiful too, but none more so than mine, for we had Old Baldy.

Old Baldy was a big piece of hillside, long stripped clean of trees, jutting out into the center of town like my grandpa's shiny forehead. From my house I could run out the back door, across the creek, and up through the pine grove at the base of the hill. Fifteen minutes later, huffing and puffing, I'd be standing at the most magnificent spot in the world.

From here my town looked exactly like the postcards at Hamlin's Five and Dime, but you didn't have to pay even a nickel for the view. From here tiny cars drove slowly out of town on rolling country roads. From here the Pennsylvania Railroad, like a Lionell model, snaked its path along the river on its way to unload at the glass factory. From here, barely discernible from so high, children on bicycles wove their way to the swimming pool each hot summer afternoon.

It was a magical place, and from the age of five I went there often. Sometimes I went alone. Sometimes I went with a friend, and often on summer nights with a whole pack of buddies. We carried our sleeping bags and little blue boxes of Camp Fire Marshmallows, each box containing two cardboard trays, each tray containing two rows of six neatly lined white sticky treats.

As the orange sun dropped into a distant forest, we would watch the miniature street lamps below blinking on like strings of tiny lights on a Christmas tree. Above us through the clean air, the stars were obscured only by the bright haze of their own blazing glory.

In the winter we tobogganed down Baldy's icy face, six little blue-lipped buddies, laced together, holding on to one another's frozen buckled boots, screaming at the top of our lungs.

In the late summer, lying on sleds of flattened cardboard boxes, we careened down its grassy front, rolling off before Baldy's leafy hairline of tiny seedlings.

Old Baldy was just a big piece of grassy hillside in the center of my little town, but it played a big part in my growing up. I took my first solo hike there as a five-year-old. I had my first campout there at eight. I met my first "date" up there when I was thirteen (it beat being driven somewhere by my folks). I took my fiancé there when I was twenty.

But the most special times on Baldy, the times that have had a lasting effect (even down to my own children), were the times I spent with my dad. One of my first vivid memories is of a Sunday afternoon one November, a day of frosty breath, my dad unthreading his skinny satin tie with a flick of the wrist. "Say, Bobby, how about a little hike up Old Baldy?"

This scene was to be repeated many times. Dad would pull on black arctics over polished dress shoes, a scratchy school letter jacket, and a wool hat. My mom would help me put on every imaginable piece of warm winter clothing, and then off we would go.

As hard as the climb was, stumbling over my own feet, sliding on the nearly frozen ground, sweating through several sweaters, I plodded upward. I wanted to get to the top. To me that was the whole idea of climbing Old Baldy, to get to the top. But my dad knew better than I. My dad knew that the whole idea was to experience the climb together.

"Hush, son," he would say, stopping by the creek or by the stand of pines or under a rusty old oak still clinging to its wrinkling dry leaves. "Stand quietly," he would whisper so softly I could hardly hear. "Listen!"

I was never sure what I was supposed to be listening for. "What, Dad?" I would snap impatiently. "I can't hear anything! What is it? Huh? What?"

"Shh," he would say in one long soft breath. "Be still and just listen. Shh."

Then, very faintly at first, I would hear it. The sighing complaint of a tall maple gently moving in a light breeze. The flourish of a black squirrel running a tightrope from tree to tree. The mournful chorus of many geese flying too high to be seen. The plinking burble of trickling water flowing between layers of melting ice. To my dad, beautiful music. In these gentle moments, as I breathed through my mitten and my toes numbed in my cramped boots, my father taught me to listen.

Of course, we would eventually reach the top. There, sitting together, I'd nuzzle in the warmth of his arms as he pointed toward the spot, far below, where we had begun, or to the very place where I had slipped near the creek, or perhaps toward the path entrance, through the pines, that would have led us on a more direct route.

Always too soon we would have to climb back down.

"Aw, please, Dad, can't we stay here just a little longer?" I'd say.

"Nope, let's go, buddy," he would reply. "Time to head back."

"Hey, Dad, I have an idea! Why don't you just build us a house up here?"

"Well, we'll see," he would chuckle. "Maybe someday."

Later, exhausted, climbing into bed after a hot bath, I would remember those quiet moments along the way. Deep inside, peace would settle into my spirit. And I would fall asleep with the faint traces of a smile still on my face.

Oh, to be sure, all my life would not be so pastoral. In my teens I would tune my more powerful receiver to stronger stations, playing much louder music. I'd continue to watch the news from the big cities. I'd hear the cacophony of crime, the din of foreign war, and the screaming protests in a park, coincidentally, not far from the Loop. I chose to listen to all the noise, and it made a difference.

As a young man it became more difficult to be quiet. To take time. Now, as an adult, I often find myself caught in the climb, wincing at the distortion of stress and the deafening pressures to be successful. Without a doubt I have changed a lot since I was that child.

But always God has remained the same. For always along the way there has been a still, small voice, one that sounds very much like my dad's, saying, "Shh! Be still ... Listen ... I have something beautiful for you to hear."

"What, Father?" I snap impatiently, "I'm busy! What is it? I don't hear anything!"

"Shh ... listen."

And then, very softly at first ... from deep within ... a long soft sigh of regret ... then a tiny rustling of hope and finally, resonating just beneath my melting facade, the warm melodic plinking burble of God's peace.

I've grown to recognize these moments as the mountaintop. For it is here that I am able to see my life in the proper perspective. It is here that I can glimpse where I began, where I have triumphed, where I have fallen or taken the wrong path. The view is so magnificent that I want to live here all the time. I cannot do that now, but I know someday I will.

Now Old Baldy is gone.

Oh, it's still there, but it's not bald anymore. Each year, the pine grove and the leafy seedlings crept higher and higher toward the top. Sadly, the last time I visited, the open bald space on top of the mountain was gone. But the lessons I learned there live on.

"Hey, buddy," I called to my youngest last Thanksgiving morning, "how about a little hike up Old Baldy?"

Lars fiddled with his Walkman. Yanking the earplugs out of his head, he said, "What did you say, Dad?"

"Go ask your grandpa if he wants to take a little hike with us up on Old Baldy."

Ten minutes later, Lars leading the way, the three of us crossed the freezing creek now deep within a tall canopy of pine.

Suddenly my son froze still, alert. "Hey, Grandpa," he said, holding out his hand in a halting position. "Grandpa," he whispered so softly we could hardly hear. And then, in one long breath, "Shh ... listen ..."

My father, pulling his wool cap off his good ear, tipped his head to the side.

Faintly at first, and then more strongly, we heard above us a melancholy sound.

A tender smile lit my father's face. Putting a hand on his grandson's shoulder, he gazed up through the gray branches.

"Ah ..." he whispered. "Geese!"

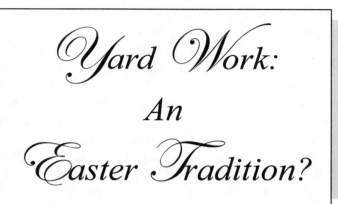

CHAPTER 5

Yard Work: An Easter Tradition?

Jerusalem, about A.D. 30

The area was secure. Within the tomb, on a stone slab, the carcass lay cold. A rock blocked the entrance, and Roman soldiers, the best in the business, stood vigilant outside. Anyone attempting to steal the body would face them first, fierce fighters, ready to die.

Ironically, all the security was unnecessary, for no thief, human or spectral, would enter this cave and survive. You see, angels were everywhere, and they had orders too. They stood, rows of them, beside, beneath, and above the body of Jesus, swords drawn, singing a swelling chorus of anticipation, wings fluttering a soft percussion. The body of Jesus would not be stolen. His Father had seen to it. The area was secure.

How strange to think that no one heard the musical climax. No one heard the brassy blast of light piercing the darkness. No one saw the celestial warriors rocketing into battle. No one saw the morning stars flicker and then disappear in the arc of white light. No one saw lasers severing the foul chains of hell, melting metal like hot knives through clay. No one heard or saw a thing, no one.

The disciples would have loved to witness the event. They weren't busy. They weren't even sleeping in these early morning hours. Two nights earlier they had been unable to stay awake even when Jesus begged them to wait and watch with him. Now they wondered if they would ever sleep soundly again, so dark was their grief.

If they'd only known what was happening at the tomb they would have been there. But they weren't invited. How strange that no one was.

It was the brightest moment in history—the brightest moment since God spoke light into being. Yet no one knew, and in eternity God savored the secret. He might have announced his great triumph with an earthquake, lightning flashing across the sky, and winds ripping up trees by the roots. He might have spoken from heaven a mighty "I told you so!" But quietly he savored the moment, awaiting an appropriate herald.

The first sunlight lit the eastern sky, and as staggering soldiers fled in fear, a woman approached the tomb. It was she whom God awaited. It was she who found that Jesus was gone. It was she who first mistook the shepherd for a gardener and then ran to her friends shouting, "He is risen!"

She spoke the words—and the world would never be the same.

About 2,000 Years Later, Lower Mundane

I awakened to the sound of bells ringing from our Old White Church on the hillside. My red digital alarm displayed four minutes past six. From my pillow, through squinting eyes, I watched the first rays of morning light glint through dirty wintered panes, and I counted the bells. Ten, eleven, twelve … I knew they'd only begun … twenty-three, twenty-four.

Last year I'd been asked to sing at the Easter sunrise service in Hillside Cemetery. I'd stood in a chilling sleet, a green garbage bag over my guitar … thirty-one, thirty-two, thirty-three. Then too, I'd counted … Forty-eight, forty-nine. About two dozen people had shown up, including my friend Pastor Ryan Care, whose idea it was to have a community-wide, ecumenical sunrise service … Seventy, seventy-one.

Ryan loves Jesus passionately—just a little more than he loves creativity. It was his idea to ring the bells one time for each year since the first Easter.

"There are many people right here in town who don't know about Easter morning," he told his church board. "My question to you is, How are we going to tell them that Jesus is alive?"

Apparently the sunrise service was the last item on a long agenda at the March monthly board meeting. It was late, and people, being tired and anxious to get home, said, "Pastor, you go ahead and plan the service. That's what you're good at. That's what we pay you for."

Of the two dozen folks who showed up in the early morning darkness, most were old folks, including Winifred

Rossi, who turns ninety-four this July. She was accompanied by her sons, Ross and Russel, and Father Schiller from St.Theresa's.

The cemetery is right next to the Old White Church, and the newly installed electronic bells are deafening even at half volume … 206, 207 … but for this special service, Ryan had turned them way up … 294, 295. The bells had been ringing for more than five minutes. The old folks held leather gloves over their ears, which helped only a little. Ryan stood, head bowed, apparently in prayer … 700 … 701 … 702 … 703.

From where I stood it looked as if Winifred were weeping. From the hillside you could see lights beginning to flicker in bedroom windows down near the river. 1217 … 1218. Winifred had to be taken to her car. Father Schiller came over to Ryan and, with no attempt to hide his anger, shouted, "My congregation will not participate next year if *you* have anything to do with it." He stormed away. 1465 … 1466.

I was freezing. About half the crowd headed to the warmth of their cars to wait it out. Several pulled away.

After about half an hour, sometime between the years of Columbus and the Spanish Inquisition, I saw the blue lights of the police cruiser racing up Hillside Avenue … 1536, 1537. Deputy Joey Buford, a son of Lower Mundane, walked straight up to Ryan and, with his face only inches away, shouted point blank, "Stop the noise now, Pastor, or I'm hauling you all in!"

At this point that would mean only three of us. Most of the cars had pulled away when they saw the flashing lights.

Ryan, blue-lipped, head soaked, and looking just a little frightened, finally realized he should have listened to his wife, Janine, when she had asked, "Are you sure you've thought this one through?"

He had responded, "Honey, I don't know if it'll mean anything to anyone, but maybe it's a beginning."

Now he shouted over the din of his creativity, "Five more minutes, Joey. They're on a timer. Give me five more minutes!"

Six minutes later the bells stopped, and without a word to either of us, shaking his head in disgusted incredulity, Joey Buford climbed into his cruiser and pulled away. Ryan said I didn't need to sing since the service was sort of over anyway.

Now I lay in my bed on Easter morning a year later and thankfully heard the bells stop at sixty. I had an excuse this year. I'd been gone over the weekend and hadn't reached home until 2:30. I'd told Ryan I wouldn't be able to make it.

Lying nestled in my bed, I felt good. I imagined Ryan preaching to the few who dared to show up a second year, guessing Father Schiller was not one of them.

But I was bothered that Ryan's question remained unanswered. How *are* we going to tell people that Jesus is alive? He was right. So many people here in Lower Mundane don't know that he has risen.

This fact was made clear several hours later on the way to church. We'd decided to attend the nine o'clock service and then go for Easter brunch at DeLuca's on Old County Road H near the airport. As usual, on the way to church we stopped by the Old Corner Store to pick up a Sunday paper.

I ought to mention that I don't often wear a tie, and I didn't even own a suit until I opened the closet this Easter morning and found that Judy had been shopping for me while I was gone. There, still in the plastic bag, was a beautiful new suit.

"Save the tags," she said. "If you don't like it or if it doesn't fit, we can take it back."

Well, it did fit, and I did like it, and shortly thereafter, looking better than I'd looked at my own wedding, I walked into the Old Corner Store to get a Sunday paper. The store, like almost everything else in town, is owned by Winifred Rossi. But Donny Barnes manages it. Donny's about my age. He looks as though he's lived a rough life, and I know for a fact that after his long days behind the counter he often spends a few more hours with the boys down at Tooters Bar and Grill.

When we first moved here, he didn't have much to say to me. This was probably because, since his prices were so high, I rarely bought more than the paper or maybe a couple of doughnuts. Over the months, though, he had loosened up a bit and usually had something approaching a smile in response to my greeting.

This morning when I walked in to get my paper, Donny looked me up and down and whistled. "Woo-Whee!" he said, "Will you look at those duds."

Glancing around, I was relieved to find the store empty except for the two of us.

"Well, thanks," I said, tossing my seventy-five cents on the counter and reaching for a paper. "Just a little surprise gift from my wife." I started to leave.

"I guess so!" he said, leaning over the counter to inspect my shoes. "So what's the special occasion?"

"What do you mean?" I asked.

"I mean, why are you all dressed up?"

"It's Easter," I said.

He didn't say, "Oh, by golly it is! Can you imagine that? I forgot." He didn't say, "Well I know that, but since when do you wear a suit to church?" He didn't say a thing. His expression did not change in the least. He stared at me as if he didn't understand the words, as if I'd spoken in a foreign language. "See you next week," he said.

I think the service was wonderful, but I can't say so with certainty because I wasn't as present as I wanted to be. I spent most of the time reconstructing my conversation at the Old Corner Store. Sadly I suspected Donny didn't even know what Easter was.

After church we had an excellent brunch. Judy and I ordered the buffet, and much to their mom's distress, the boys once again ordered burgers.

"Come on, you guys," she protested. "This is a beautiful restaurant, and it's Easter. Can't you, just once, order something nice?"

"It *is* nice, Mom," they countered. "The Supah DeLucah costs almost as much as your buffet."

After cheesecake and coffee, we headed back home. It was a beautiful day, unusually warm and sunny, the kind of rare, early spring afternoon in which you can imagine the sound of birds returning, in which you can almost envision new, leafy buds dusting the riverside forest with a hazy green. But signs of winter carnage remained: gray yards covered with sticks, piles of snow-plowed gravel, and souvenirs from the neighbors' dogs.

Within minutes the boys had made phone calls, changed into hooded sweatshirts, and shot out the door to find their friends.

"So," Judy said, "you probably feel like taking a nap, don't you?"

"Well, no," I said. "If it weren't Easter, I'd like nothing more than to spend the afternoon cleaning up the lawn."

It sounded strange to hear myself saying the words. When I was growing up, my dad refused to do any kind of work on Sunday. He didn't want to be a poor witness. The neighbors could mow, rake, paint, and retar their roofs if they wanted to, but *we* didn't work on the Sabbath.

Now, however, I not only wanted to do yard work on the Sabbath, but I also wanted to do it on Easter Sunday. Of course, I would do it as quietly as possible, not doing anything that involved power machinery. I just wanted to do a little raking, maybe plant the bulbs we had stored in the cellar. I wanted to experience this beautiful day, and I couldn't think of a more fulfilling way to do it.

"Why, Bob Stromberg," Judy gasped contemptuously. "Clean the yard on Easter Sunday?"

I started to defend myself, but she cut me off with a wink. "That's exactly what I was thinking."

For the next four hours we worked hard—raking, piling, planting, occasionally taking a break to toss our boys the first Frisbee of the season. I even got out some house paint and touched up the latticework around the front porch. I took down the storm windows, and Judy began to wash the streaked tear stains of winter condensation from the inside panes.

A few older folks from church drove by and waved, probably wondering about our spirituality, but that was okay. If they were concerned, then they simply didn't understand.

Surprisingly, I felt we were beginning to experience Easter. Before our eyes all that was dead or filthy began to disappear. The lawn was cleaned. The hardened, dead flower beds were broken apart, tilled, and prepared for the life that would soon burst out of them—life that would sound forth whether we took the time to listen or not.

For some reason this Easter we were invited to participate through hard work and recreation.

As I finished near the end of the driveway and shoveled the last pile of refuse into the wheelbarrow, Judy approached with a hot cup of coffee. Her cheeks were rosy, her hair pulled back with a kerchief, her left hand propped into the small of her sore lower back.

"Oh," she said painfully, joyful, "I'm exhausted. What a wonderful day!"

As we stood with our backs to the road, surveying our good work, a vehicle pulled up behind us. Turning, we saw Donny Barnes reaching across the front seat of his old pickup and rolling down the window.

Smiling, he asked, "Little early for spring cleaning, isn't it?"

"Oh, do you think so?" I said.

"Well, it's just that you're the first ones. And I'll tell you it looks real fine too. This morning I wouldn't have imagined your yard could look this good."

"Thanks," I said. "It feels nice."

"So is this an Easter tradition with you or what?"

"You know what, Donny?" Judy said, "It was never an Easter tradition before, but I think maybe it should be from now on."

"Not a bad idea," he said, still smiling. "If everyone adopted it, this town would look a whole lot better every spring."

"Well, not only that" I said, "but hey, this is what Easter is all about."

I looked at him closely and guessed he didn't make any spiritual connections. How could he have? I may have given him the idea Easter is some kind of gardening day internationally celebrated by church people—I'm not sure. It probably wasn't much of a witness, but as Pastor Ryan would say, "Maybe it was a beginning."

Still smiling, Donny said, "Have a good one," and drove off.

CHAPTER 6

Dollars in the Dumpster

Pete Mundy has delivered the mail in Lower Mundane since the town incorporated in 1939. According to all the old folks, he wasn't much faster then than he is now. As a mail carrier, Pete has three problems—besides the fact that he can hardly walk anymore. He loves food, he loves conversation, and he loves his old friends.

Fully one-third of his deliveries are to folks even older than he. Many of them can no longer see well and have trouble reading, so they invite Pete in for a cup of coffee and a little chat. Before long his feet are up by the fireplace, bifocals on his nose, and a six-page letter in his hands. Only when the last piece of junk mail is opened and discarded will he continue on to the next home. By the time he arrives at our house we're usually eating supper.

When I first moved to town, I tried to complain to the postmaster. I was told sharply, "We're well aware of the problem, but nothing's going to change until Pete retires in

June. Lots of old folks depend on him. He's' been a faithful public servant for fifty years, and you just don't fire someone like that."

I never suggested Pete be fired. I just wanted to receive my mail during normal business hours. Judging from the postmaster's reaction, though, apparently I'd broken some ordinance prohibiting newcomers from criticizing the mailman.

Maybe the old folks loved Pete, but to me he seemed inefficient and often downright cantankerous. One late winter afternoon I spoke to him briefly on my front porch.

"Mr. Mundy," I said as sweetly as possible, "I know how busy you are, and I'm sure I don't want to make your job any more difficult than it is, but I'm having a little problem."

Pete stopped sorting my mail and shifted his nearly empty, old cracked leather delivery bag further back on his hip. But he did not look at me. In fact, it seemed like he didn't hear me.

I tried again. "Again, I hope you understand I'm sure not complaining," I continued. "It's just that I'm having some difficulty with my correspondence, and it would really be helpful, in fact, I'd be thrilled, if I could receive my mail a little earlier. Actually anytime before five."

"And I'd be thrilled to do that for you." Pete said, lifting his face, smiling oddly and peering overtop of his bifocals.

"Oh, well, that's wonderful," I said with a chuckle, relieved to have the conversation over. But Pete wasn't through.

"Yes, sir, young man," he said, still smiling but with anger creeping into his voice. "Yes, sir, I'd be thrilled to deliver your mail earlier. And I would too. But ... " He walked past me and dropped my letter in the porch box. "You see, unfortunately I'm doing my very best to serve the people of Lower Mundane. Especially the people who have given their whole lives to make this a great place for you to live."

I tried to interrupt. "No, no. Listen, you must misunderstand me. I just—"

"Don't go thinkin' for a minute that you can come in here and change us all overnight," he scolded. "If you don't like the way we do things, then maybe you ought to move back where you came from." With that he turned and walked away.

I didn't get it. I didn't ask to have my mail delivered in the morning or even before lunch. I said five o'clock. Every sinew of reason screamed that I had a right to feel angry. What kind of public servant was this old man?

On the other hand, I knew he would be carrying my mail daily until June, and if I aggravated him further, I risked not receiving it at all. Repeatedly thereafter, for purposes practical as well as spiritual, I tried to mend the relationship, but Pete refused to help.

Then one day, while Judy and I sat eating lunch, the doorbell rang. It was Pete. He handed me a bundle and spoke fast without making eye contact.

"Somethin' from the PTO in there, some kind of form letter. Other than that it's all junk. Sorry 'bout what I said last month. I'm redoing my route—should be able to get here a little earlier. Sweep your snowy steps or you're going to find your mail on top of the garbage can." Having said his piece, he turned and hobbled away.

Well, I guess if that was his way of saying "I'm sorry," then I certainly would accept the apology.

Just as he said, the mail was mostly junk, and there *was* a form letter from the Parent-Teachers Organization, though even that was of no great interest. I had been expecting it and already knew its contents. In fact, at 2:00 A.M. the Sunday before, after I crawled out of a university dumpster, I had suggested the letter be written as soon as possible. I made the suggestion to Janine Care, the fund-raising director for the PTO's playground committee.

Now, before I explain what I was doing crawling around in a dumpster at 2:00 in the morning, I need to fill you in on a few details.

Two months ago, Janine Care was asked to head the committee to raise money for a new playground. Let me say she did not seek this position. She even fumed a little when the PTO president asked if she would be willing to help. She complained to Judy, "The only reason they always call me is because I don't happen, at the time, to have a job *or* a baby. I know they sit around and say, 'Oh Janine Care has nothing else to do. Why don't we just ask her?' I'll tell you, between taxiing my own kids around and helping Ryan at church, I don't even have time to wash my hair. And then what do I tell them? I say yes, I'd be happy to!"

She threw her hands above her head and huffed in exasperation. "Sometimes I amaze myself."

Though she didn't mention it to Judy, there was another reason Janine was a reluctant committee member. She and the PJTO president, Marie Soderholm, had had several previous unpleasant encounters. Marie is a perfectionist with an explosive temper and a very short fuse. Once before she had blown up at Janine for bringing strawberry instead of strawberry-rhubarb pie to a bake sale. Needless to say, Janine was not eager to work with her again.

But accept the task she did, and characteristically she attacked it with an efficiency and enthusiasm that would probably only induce the committee to call again. Janine is a tiny woman, barely five feet tall, and all her life she has had to deal with people treating her like a child. To compensate for this liability, she has cultivated a confidence and an aggressiveness that will not take no for an answer. This is hardly an asset for a pastor's wife, but it's an ideal quality for a fund-raising director.

For several years the old metal playground equipment behind the elementary school had been deteriorating. Then last spring a fourth grader named Skippy, one of the little Guncheon twins, slipped on the monkey bars and broke four front teeth. Clearly, the PTO needed to take action.

At a PTO meeting, Janine suggested they contact the Dreamscape Company of Sioux City, Iowa. Dreamscape comes into the elementary school and encourages the children to draw pictures of the most wonderful playgrounds they can imagine. Architects then incorporate many of the children's ideas into a fantastic yet safe design, built of durable, pressure-treated wood, rubber tires, and large PVC drainage pipes.

A committee then recruits the labor force from the community, drawing mainly from the parents of the children who will enjoy the playground. The construction is supervised by the company, built over a few weekends, and ideally becomes a festive, unifying community project.

Janine declared, "If we're going to build a playground, we might as well spend the money to build one that is safe, long lasting and above all something that the kids will want to play on for years to come."

Everyone agreed. Subcommittees were appointed to contact Dreamscape, recruit volunteers, and raise funds. Even with the volunteer labor, costs were projected to run near seven or eight thousand dollars. Much to her chagrin, Janine became fund-raising director.

Now, Janine is a classy woman, and we knew from the start there would be no car washes, dunk tanks, or bowlathons. Furthermore she had never bought a raffle ticket in her life. No, if Janine was the director, then the job would be done with style.

A week later everyone in town received an invitation to the Dreamscape for Kids Fund-Raising Banquet to be held in the city at the university's Alumni Hall. Everyone would have preferred to have the banquet here in town, but Janine calculated correctly that there would be far too much community interest for the elementary cafeteria to suffice. Furthermore, David Soderholm, husband to PTO chairman Marie, is an administrator at the university and was able to secure the hall and student help at a reduced rate.

Mary Ellen Borstad, a local caterer and mother of three elementary children, agreed to cater the dinner as her contribution to the project. The party store out on Old County Road H offered to provide free napkins and paper tablecloths. Janine made several persuasive calls to Dreamscape, which finally agreed to create a playground model for display in the post office lobby and at the banquet. Even I was cajoled into entertaining with a short childhood story.

The whole town was chattering about the event. Nearly everything but the cost of the food had been supplied, and it looked as though the evening would be a fabulous success.

Six hundred people showed up outside the banquet room for punch at 6:30. At seven the main doors opened. Guests were delighted to see that Lower Mundane's very own master carpenter, Eric Burt, had constructed a swinging bridge just like the one designed by their children. The adventuresome who wished to try could enter Alumni Hall over the bridge. I doubt a dozen people didn't take the challenge.

The meal was typical banquet fare, consisting of a slice of gray turkey wrapped around a scoop of stuffing and topped with a squiggle of tepid gravy, but no one complained. People were excited to be there, and I sensed they were ready to contribute.

My part in the program went well enough for a freebie, and several women from our local Sweet Adelines sang some acceptable barbershop. But the evening's highlight came with the appearance of the two little Guncheon twins, Skippy and Chippy. You remember that Skippy is the boy who broke all his front teeth on the old playground set.

The boys were surprise guests. No one, including the fund-raising committee, knew they were coming. They just showed up with their parents, who looked up Janine prior to the meal. In a truly ecumenical act, Janine had just escorted Father Schiller over the swinging bridge. When she stepped from the bridge into the banquet hall, she was confronted with the twins and their parents, Frank and Florida Guncheon.

"It is so nice to meet you, Janine." Florida said a little too loudly, taking Janine's hand in her manly grip and shaking it excessively. Florida is one of the tallest people in town. She is nearly six foot four inches, even in her fifteen-year-old earth shoes, which she wore inelegantly beneath a jean skirt and a Detroit Pistons T-shirt.

"I'm Florida," she said with a large toothy smile. Gesturing over top of Janine's head toward the bridge, she added, "And that's my husband, Frank."

Janine turned to see a long-haired trollish man, in a brown corduroy suit, crouching beneath the swinging bridge. He looked back toward the women with an impish smile and motioned them to be quiet. To Janine's dismay, Pross and Katherine Worthy, two of her older friends, were about to make their way over the bridge, which now had a giggling troll parked beneath it.

"Oh, Frank, knock it off!" Florida shouted.

Still grinning, Frank crawled out from beneath the bridge as Florida reached down and put one long hand on Janine's shoulder. With the other she motioned toward her little twins. "I'd like you to meet our two boys, Skippy and Chippy. They have a few words they'd like to share in the program tonight concerning the importance of safer playground equipment."

Janine was hesitant to say yes because everyone knows that the Guncheons are a little … well … *different*. When they first moved to town last year, they painted an eight-foot happy face on the side of their new brick home. On Halloween Frank dressed up like a bat and hung upside down on the front porch. After the big February snowstorm, the family built a snow cave in the backyard and lived outside for a month. During a week of summer vacation they rented a room eighteen miles away at the Chastain Midtown Motel and ate three meals a day at the new Arby's. No one else in town had ever done any of those things.

Had Janine asked the boys exactly what they were going to say they probably would not have gotten the opportunity. But there they stood, cute as could be, all dressed up in their white shirts and ties, looking as identical as each of our six hundred turkey rolls.

Janine asked sweetly if they were sure they could keep it to two minutes, and the boys nodded. Each held a three-by-five card and was obviously well prepared, so Janine made the judgment call and put them on the program.

An hour later, the two boys skipped hand in hand down the center aisle and crawled up onto the platform. "Friends of Lower Mundane," one of the boys said like a little politician, "my name is Skippy Guncheon, and this is my twin brother, Chippy." He stiffly held out a hand, indicating his replica. "No, wait a minute," he said as if truly perplexed, "I guess *I'm* Chippy, and *he's* Skippy."

It was a rim shot one-liner he had undoubtedly presented countless times in his nine years, and it worked again to perfection. Everyone howled.

"You probably wonder how my mom and dad can tell us apart," he continued with a toothy smile, again pointing toward his sibling. "Well, actually, we don't look that much alike anymore."

His brother, Skippy, then smiled an equally large grin.

A gasp rose from the tables. This youngster, who only seconds before had been a darling duplicate, suddenly looked monstrous, with each of his front teeth filed to hideously sharp points like an over-endowed juvenile vampire.

Little Skippy, who had worn temporary caps for half a year, had coincidentally had them removed that very day. The dentist was prepared to adhere the permanent caps immediately, but when Florida saw how horrid her son looked, she scheduled an appointment for the following week—after the fund-raising banquet.

Skippy held his card before him and said one little sentence. "Ladieth and gentlemen, pleath don't let thith happen again. Give to Dreamthcape for Kidth."

Only a peculiar mind like Florida Guncheon's would have thought of this tactic, but it could not have been more effective. As the boys left the platform, holding hands and waving, everyone gave them a standing ovation.

Then Janine made the financial pitch, and the women's quartet sang another number as couples conferred quietly about what their contributions should be. I didn't see anyone who wasn't writing a check or at least stuffing a few twenty-dollar bills into the envelopes and placing them on the tables.

At the dismissal Janine and five other women on the committee went out into the lobby to thank people for coming. Student help from the university began to clear tables, and Ryan Care and I decided to help Eric disassemble his swinging bridge.

Twenty minutes later we returned from carrying the last six-by-six to Eric's truck. The tables had already been set for breakfast. A custodian vacuumed a final corner of the carpet, and the committee waved good-bye to the last guest. Already the new playground had begun to unify our community.

I watched PTO president, Marie Soderholm, as she let out a tired "Whew!" and embraced Janine. Such an expression of appreciation was uncharacteristic of Marie, but it seemed genuine and certainly appropriate.

Marie stood back and held Janine at arms' length. "Well, my dear," she said, "you did a marvelous job. Thank you, thank you, thank you! Now, everyone ..." She released Janine and addressed the other women, "Let's go count the money!"

There was a pleasant tired pause of about two seconds as the committee turned to walk back into the banquet hall. Then all the bodies stopped in mid-stride, heads turned impulsively to ogle each other's horrified expressions, and everyone screamed in unison, "The money!"

They bolted as a pack into Alumni Hall, where an unfortunate college student was placing a napkin at the last breakfast setting. The poor kid never had a chance. Marie was on him in a frenzy, her hands gripped tightly around his skinny neck, shoving him against the wall.

With eyes wide in rage, the very likeness of Hitchcockian hysteria, she screamed, "What did you do with our money?!"

"What money?" the boy choked, trying to push her away.

"The money in the tablecloths!" she screamed, tightening her grip.

"They were paper," he squawked. "We rolled them up and threw them away."

She dropped him to the floor like a rag. Within seconds we were outdoors behind the kitchen, staring at three large dumpsters. Two of them were filled with stained paper table rolls and many uneaten balls of turkey. Unfortunately the third container had just been emptied into a garbage truck, and the operator insisted it couldn't be dumped back out. Fortunately it was his last stop, and he wasn't able to hail it away until the next morning anyway, so he agreed to leave it there overnight. He locked up the cab and opened up the top of the container so Ryan, Eric and I could climb within and salvage what we could.

It wasn't our responsibility, but we felt we should help. Besides, David Soderholm, the only other man to witness his wife's attack, had sheepishly left without a word.

From our vantage point atop the truck, we looked beneath as Marie went into a dumpster like a soldier into a foxhole, tossing turkey rolls like hand grenades, screaming, cursing, weeping. Janine climbed in behind her. Ryan peered below, prepared to leap to his wife's defense should Marie snap her last tiny thread to sanity. I could tell by Ryan's expression he was concerned Marie might lose it at any moment.

At 2:45 A.M. we shoved the last soggy check into a manila envelope, quite certain we had retrieved most of the contributions. Of course we couldn't be sure.

Ryan offered to drive Marie home, which was a mistake. Climbing into her car, she glowered with an expression that suggested a sour taste had risen in the back of her throat. "I am perfectly capable of driving myself," she said, and squealed away.

Before we left, I suggested that Janine write a simple letter to all who had attended the banquet, apologizing for the inconvenience and explaining without too much detail what had happened. She wrote it well and even asked that, if people failed to receive canceled bank checks, would they please consider writing another contribution. The letter was gracious, professional, and about as good as it could be.

Typically, Marie insisted that Janine sign the letter herself, not on behalf of the committee. It was small of Marie to suggest it and big of Janine to concede.

Even with the mishap the evening was a great success and nearly all the money was raised. I talked to Ryan earlier today, and he said that Janine, now a month later, is beginning to put it all into perspective. As far as I can tell, the townspeople have been remarkably gracious. There is little doubt that very soon the children of Lower Mundane will have a beautiful new playground.

Mari Soderholm, however, remains embarrassed or embittered or something. I ran into her yesterday at the Old Corner Store. She stood at the checkout counter paying Donny Barnes for a small bag of groceries.

"So, Marie," I teased, "you been keepin' yourself out of the garbage these days?"

I felt I had the right to speak like a friend. After all, I'd been there too. I'd crawled around in turkey gravy and ruined my new suit pants. But apparently poor Marie was still fuming about the incident. "Don't get me going!" she snipped. "I still can't believe anyone could be so stupid as to allow that to happen. Thousand of dollars thrown in the garbage! From now on I handle these fund-raisers myself." She turned and walked out the door.

Donny Barnes looked at me, and together we burst into laughter. Not because Marie was funny, but because Marie had left her groceries sitting on the counter. I reached for the bag, thinking I could catch her, but Donny stopped me.

"No, no," he said, "Give her a minute. She'll be back."

Sure enough, before I'd paid for my goods, the car returned, and a red-faced Marie walked back in. Without a hint of humor she said, "I believe you have something that belongs to me."

Poor Marie. She doesn't get it. She doesn't realize that what happened to her and what happened to Janine is an everyday occurrence. Dumb mistakes are an occupational hazard of this job called life. Many times we get so distracted by peripheral activities that we fail to accomplish or even recognize our central purpose. We don't quite finish what we came to do, so all our efforts are rendered fruitless.

Was Janine's task to raise funds? No, not really. Her task was to raise funds *and* collect them, *and* give them to the committee to build a playground. She did a great job. She just got a little distracted and didn't quit finish.

And then there's the postal worker Pete Mundy. It's hard for me to be critical of him. After all, he serves the older people of Lower Mundane in a beautiful way. He visits with them, makes them a cup of tea, even shovels their steps if necessary, and for all this he is greatly loved. But is that his job? Well, no, not if you ask the United States Postal Department. They'll tell you his job is to deliver the mail. They'll tell you even good things like relationships can be peripheral distractions.

I happen to believe that Pete's central purpose really *is* serving others, and I suspect he will continue to do that even better after he retires. But I agree with his employer too. Unfortunately Pete's purpose has never complemented his vocation. He has only performed one well.

The apostle Paul said, "I consider my life worth nothing to me, if only I may finish the race and complete the task the Lord Jesus has given me" (Acts 20:24). He knew that the task of testifying to God's grace was a tough one, a grueling marathon that would claim his very life. But he recognized that in the end, staying with the task and finishing the race was the most important thing.

How magnificent to be like that, to clearly know one's purpose and live with a focus and determination to see it completed. God has given us all the time we need to finish. How sad it would be to arrive at the end of life distracted. How sad to discover all the fruit of our labor thrown into the garbage.

Marie stood beside me and waited for Donny to answer.

"Well," he said, searching behind the counter, "I don't think I have anything of yours." Then his eyes widened in fake surprise. "No, wait a minute. I'm sorry. By golly! I do!" He handed her the bag.

Apparently failing to see any irony, Marie turned and, without a word, walked away.

CHAPTER 7

My *Problem* of *Joy*

Joy is the simplest form of gratitude.

Karl Barth

My carpenter buddy Eric Burt stopped by today to check out the damage. He started upstairs in my son Nathan's room by stretching some clear plastic over the broken window. Then he examined the carpet, which is probably going to be okay. Apparently there's some kind of product that can remove algae stains. Then he went downstairs and inspected the living room ceiling and the plasterboard beneath the peeling paper on the north wall.

"Amazing," he said, unable to hide his amusement, "how one little golf ball could cause all this."

"Yeah, well, it did," I said, acting a little more perturbed than I really was. I had had a couple of days to cool off.

Eric stripped a long, thin piece of wallpaper from the ceiling right down to the baseboard. It lay over his hand, wet and pasty like pasta.

"Amazing," he repeated, shaking his head. "Reminds me of some of the river homes after the flood of '72. What was he using?"

"What do you mean what was he using? What was who using?"

"Nathan. What was he using? Was it a seven or a nine iron? Had to be a nine. No way he could have hit that ball so high with a seven. Unless he hit it from out in the street."

"Well, that's not what he told me," I answered, not really interested in what kind of club it was. "He said he hit it from the flower bed. Just a nice little chip shot."

Eric let loose a laugh that only yesterday would have seemed insensitive. "No way it was a nice little chip," he said, mimicking the shot by dipping his knee and swinging his tape measure into the carpet. "He had some power on that ball. If it hadn't gone through the window, it would have sailed clear down to Arnold Avenue. I'll tell you, Bob, you should be proud. That kid's going to be a fine golfer!"

"No, Eric, I doubt that," I sniggered. "He may not live long enough to get very good."

"Well, this ought to do it," he said, scribbling an estimate and handing me the piece of paper. "Unless you want me to recaulk the aquarium."

"No," I said, inspecting the surprisingly low total, "all the fish are dead now anyway. At least all the expensive ones. I think we'll put the aquarium away for a while."

"Amazing." He chuckled. "He must have really cranked that thing. I mean, to go through the window and still crack a hole in the aquarium." Another laugh escaped, a longer one this time, and Eric covered his face. "How many gallons did it hold?" he asked, wiping his eyes.

"Seventy-five," I answered, "I think we lost about seventy-four."

I walked with Eric down the driveway, and he laughed pretty much the whole way. By the time we reached his truck, he had regained some composure, but when he glanced from the flower bed to the upstairs bedroom window, he lost it again.

I didn't mind, because Eric Burt is becoming a good friend, and I was overjoyed to hear him laugh. Overjoyed! Laughing is not something this intense man is inclined to do often. I had known him a long time before I had heard him so much as chuckle.

I met Eric when I first came to town. My realtor gave me his number when he saw me leaning toward having a home built instead of buying one from her.

She spoke to me, playfully glancing from side to side, as if someone might be watching. "It's not wise in this town to express a preference for any particular builder." She whispered. "But if you want your home built right, on time, and on budget, then you'd better call Eric."

So I did.

He turned out to be a fascinating guy. In the early seventies, he attended law school at U.C. Berkeley, number two in his class. He studied for three full years, and then, after all the money and hard work, three weeks before graduation, he was kicked out for cheating.

"It almost killed my folks," he told me, unable to hide the pain still evident after nearly twenty years "I made a really bad decision to help a classmate, and it cost me my career. I could have gone back after a year, but I just never got to it." Then he added, "It was really painful."

We spoke in the unfinished kitchen, still a forest of bare vertical two-by-fours, as the January wind rattled the stretched plastic that shielded us from the bitter cold outside. Eric, crawling on his knees, spoke through a smile of nails lined neatly between his teeth, the whole time pounding the kitchen sub-flooring, his every movement a lesson in efficiency.

"So you left law school to become a carpenter," I said.

"Well, not exactly," he mumbled, swiping a nail from his mouth. "I left law school because I had to. But … yeah, I guess that's the way it ended up."

"So do you like it?" I asked.

"You mean carpentry?" he answered, sitting down for a moment to rest his knees. "Yeah, I guess I like it. I like this part anyway." He smiled quickly, but then a shadow crossed his face. "Some parts of this business I could do without. Some of it's really hard."

Despite a certain darkness, I liked him. He was smart, honest; he worked hard and was very good at his craft. For some reason, though, I sensed from the beginning that Eric did not trust me. It wasn't the distrust I felt from some of the older folks, the kind that stems from my being born in a different location and generation. Eric was my age and grew up near Minneapolis, so we were in the same lower caste of recent transplants. No, the problem seemed more personal.

Since he had never said he didn't trust me, I found it awkward asking if some problem might exist. After all, we hardly had a relationship. Who was I to suggest we ought to be better friends?

On the other hand, I liked him, and I knew that I felt uncomfortable about something.

While Eric was building the house, most of the time my family and I were living in the city. Of course we were always eager to see how things were coming along, so we often would pile in the car and head out to Lower Mundane. It was during one of these jaunts, early in the spring, that I decided to have a word with Eric.

When we arrived, the house was alive with activity. The dry wallers were sanding on the main floor, the painters staining woodwork above, and the landscapers planting dogwood in warm, sunny April beds. I found Eric out back finishing a piece of trim where the back deck would be someday.

"Say, you have a minute?" I asked cheerily.

"Sure," he said pleasantly enough, making me wonder if the problem was all my imagination. He put down his hammer and sat on a sawhorse.

"Listen," I said nervously, "I want you to know that I really appreciate the great job you've done here."

"Yeah," he chuckled, "and now you're going to tell me you appreciate it, but you just don't have the money to pay me. Right?"

It was the first time I'd heard him approach a real laugh. I was beginning to consider aborting this conversation, but I heard myself stumbling on.

"No, no, you'll get paid. I just want you to know that I appreciate you and, ah … I just want you to know that I also … ah … It's probably nothing, but sometimes I've sensed some tension or something between us."

It was more a question that a statement, but Eric didn't respond. He stared at his old boots and waited for me to go on.

"Well, anyway," I said, trying to back off, "I just want you to know that I'm sorry if I've done anything to cause you to distrust me. It's probably just my misunderstanding."

I thought he might act surprised or perhaps apologize, saying, "No, no. There's no problem. I must have been preoccupied with my work, and you read me wrong." But Eric just sat, staring at his boots.

After a long pause, still unable to look me in the eye, he spoke. "You're just a mystery to me." He shook his head. "I mean, I don't understand you at all."

I'm not sure what I was expecting him to say, but it sure wasn't this. I was blindsided. I mean, what was there not to understand? We hardly knew each other. We had rarely even had a conversation that didn't include cost per square feet.

"It's your whole approach to life." He continued, his intensity building. "It just really makes me uncomfortable."

Now it was my turn to stare at my shoes and shake my head, because I began to understand where this conversation was going, and I no longer welcomed it.

Eric was on his feet, pacing back and forth, rubbing his furrowed brow, finding his verbal stride, looking just a little like the lawyer he might have become.

"Listen, Bob, for me life is a job. Right? I mean, it's always been difficult. But you just seem to smile on through. I'm not saying you're faking it. It's just ..." He paused, searching for the worlds. Then throwing his arms in the air, he blustered, "I don't get it!"

I don't remember exactly what I said at this point. I just remember feeling frustrated and mildly depressed. You see, this was not the first time I'd heard this kind of talk. No, it's the same old record, stuck in the same old scratchy groove.

You see, I understand Eric's confusion. I really do. I've had to struggle with this "joy thing" all my life.

Like Eric, I'm a child of the sixties, a decade of great social revolution, communal celebration, and self-discovery. But in many respects, a decade not characterized by joy. Though I just missed out on all the burnings, rallies, and marches, I was affected by the fallout. During those impressionable years, I knew I was supposed to be struggling with my identity, searching the lonely landscape of my soul for peace and purpose in life. I tried.

I bought some beads and sat cross-legged in sensitivity sessions, trying hard to dig up any dirt I could find. Following the example of others, some who truly were courageous, I tried to talk about deep hurts from my childhood, the horrible things I'd supposedly repressed. With the encouragement of my entire generation, I tried to remove the facade and take off the mask that hid the frightened child within. But frankly, I always felt a bit inadequate in these groups. I always felt as if my painful experiences were not quite, well, painful. Still, I tried.

I remember one group session I finally broke through and choked out the devastating truth. In a fetal position with clenched teeth I shared how my parents had refused to give me a motorcycle on my sixteenth birthday. I shared how my mom had said flatly, "We don't have any money, and besides, we don't want this birthday to be your last."

It was during this time that I first began to notice the blank expressions of confusion and disbelief from other group members. Still I tried to fit in. I tried to be miserable, but I couldn't pull it off. My face kept betraying me with happy little freckles and an oversized smile. You see, it's not that I wanted to be joyous. I just couldn't help it.

So there I sat, looking like Howdy Doody at a sit-in, certain that some therapy officer would walk in off the street, point a finger at me, and say, "That's the guy. He's got joy. Get him out of here."

For a while I thought I might outgrow joy the way you outgrow acne. But when I went to college, both conditions only worsened. I wanted to major in theater, but the head of the department took one look at me and was apparently repulsed by my whole countenance. He told me straight out, "Forget about it, Stromberg. Go into nursing or something. Hospitals might be able to use a guy like you, but we don't need you in the arts.

"You see," he continued as if he knew I didn't, "true art comes from suffering, an area in which you appear to be severely handicapped. Furthermore, you're Swedish! Go ahead," he said, starting to enjoy himself, "name one Swede other than Strindberg who ever produced a great work of art."

For one brief, hopeful moment, I thought he had hit on the root of my problem. Maybe there was something in my heritage, some genetic deficiency beyond my control that made me so repulsively joyous.

But his premise was full of holes. For generations my forebears had suffered, picking pea-sized potatoes of out piles of rocks they called farmland, just to live another day. If no great works of art came from Sweden it was not for lack of suffering. It was because Swedes were too busy trying to stay alive to produce it.

I struggled on with my problem of joy. I know that some people think my problem is dishonesty. They think I fake joy as a defensive mechanism.

I had a buddy in grade school named Danny who may have had that problem. Several times a week after school Danny was beaten up. You would think this would have made him unhappy, but while he was getting beaten, he would laugh. I mean, he would laugh as if his laughter would kill him.

"Oh , please," he would howl, "this is too funny, please no!" He would have a bloody nose and some kid would be grabbing him by his hair, and Danny would be cracking up.

The truth is I really don't think Danny viewed the situation as amusing. I think he was faking it. But I don't think it was a defensive technique like some perverse possum response. No, I really think Danny used his laughter as an *offensive* weapon. You see, Danny lost all the fights, but in a way he always won. Nobody who beat him up could ever enjoy it very much.

In any case, I don't think I'm at all like Danny. I don't think that joy is a technique, defensive or offensive, for me. Joy just *is*. And I don't feel as though I'm failing to deal with the "stuff of life." I just mostly enjoy the process.

My wife, Judy, has given birth to two beautiful children. In remembering the experiences she insists that she does not associate the word *pain* with having babies.

"It was really intense at times," she says, "but I wouldn't call it a painful experience."

The truth is, both Judy and I had a ball. Not surprisingly, many young mothers (particularly those who spent three days in labor) are less than thrilled to hear about our fun little birthing parties. But none of them can accuse us of being dishonest. Most mothers would agree that when you are having a baby you are pretty much dealing with the "stuff of birth." Faking fun during the delivery is definitely ineffective.

If it makes anyone feel better, Judy is the first to acknowledge she has a high tolerance for pain. This is the woman who mistook her burst appendix for gas bubbles. But I don't think this is why she experienced so little discomfort. I think she was blessed with a total absence of fear. Through the hours of hard work, sweat, and fierce concentration, she was a picture of peace.

I don't believe my life to be charmed either. I realize pain is a part of the fabric of life, but life is not a painful experience for me. This is not a higher level of consciousness that I have somehow attained. Indeed, I deserve no credit at all. My family, my experience, my personality, and perhaps God's design, have fostered in me an atmosphere where joy flourishes, and I will not deny it.

At the same time, I know what suffering feels like, and I don't particularly enjoy it. But I don't fear it either. I believe that God, in his grace, has faithfully accepted my fear in exchange for his joy. I don't understand why. He doesn't need to do it, but he is willing to enter the mundane of my life each day and give me joy. This is a truly magnificent thing!

When deep suffering comes, as it surely will, I believe the same grace that has sustained so many others will see me through as well. In the meantime, I'm sorry if I seem so joyous; it's just that I'm having so much fun.

Eric Burt and his crew worked only six months to build that beautiful house that has become our home. That was the easy part. He's worked a lot longer to accept me as I am. Through long conversations over many cups of coffee in other people's unfinished kitchens, I've noticed the smiles coming more frequently to Eric's face.

Then today I saw him laugh until tears filled his eyes. I began to wonder if our little golfing accident may have had its hidden advantages—though I don't plan to mention that to my son. The important thing is, Eric is becoming a good friend, and that makes me very happy.

CHAPTER 8

Sunlight Smiled on the *House's Face*

On a wall in our new home, this one we had built for us, hangs a watercolor of our old home, the one we renovated ourselves. The carpenters worked *here* for four months. We labored *there* for eight years. Both were wonderful processes, but the renovation of our old home, built by a sailor long before my birth, was far more thrilling.

I wonder what God enjoys more, building or renovating? His Word begins with the creation but climaxes with redemption. All that he had made was ruined. The windows were broken, and sin reigned; ceilings and floors were rotten right to the fallen foundation. Then God's love made it beautiful again. Magnificence transformed the mundane.

I'm not surprised. That's what love does.

The watercolor of our old home is, for us, a watercolor
of love.

Sunlight smiled on the house's face
as the sailor's hands built the place
a hundred years ago or more.
And his lovely wife in frilly skirts
chased two little children in cotton shirts
out the door on sunny days to play and play and play.
And their father would say, "I love you."
And the children would shout, "Love you too, Dad.
Bye-bye!"
And with a kiss the man would taste the tears
that lay upon the face of his lovely wife
"I love you, dear, with all my life," he would say.
"Oh, how I hate to go. Do pray for me."
And off he'd go to sail the sea
again and again and again

And then …
one very dark day the man returned no more.
Soon town folks came through the house's door
dressed all in black.
Men sighed and women wept
and the children sat
looking very ill
until … at last
a month had passed
and the house stood still and empty.
For the woman and her children had left

on a day of tears and rain.
And the house felt so much love
and so much pain.

Of course, other owners eventually came
and lived within its rooms,
but somehow it was not the same.
For most by wealth were well consumed
and seldom words of love were spoken.
And like its splintered gingerbread
the town folks said,
"That house's heart is broken."
Years later, long shards of glass lay all about
from stones thrown hard each autumn
by older boys who snuck within,
without concern,
for no one ever caught them
or even cared to try.
You see, now the house was hardly seen by anyone
    at all.
Seeds soft hands so long ago had sown
now to weeds and trees had grown.
And where white paint once had shined
now all devoured by clinging vine,
the house was slowly dying.

But even when a century old,
filled with snow and grief untold
the house could still recall the joy
of the sailor and wife and girl and boy.

Yes, still
deep within its rotted wood
it could recall it all.

And then one fall day
a car parked near
and out stepped a man and a woman.
"Well, dear, what do you think?" he asked,
his arm around her waist.
"Well," she said and laughed delightedly,
"you're right, it's quite a place
but, oh my, such a lot of work!
Do you really think we should?"

And though the house was only wood
and could not say,
"Oh, yes, please come in.
Please walk through.
Imagine all that you could do!
Envision all that I could share."
No, though it could not speak,
the two *did* peek inside and
sensing something special there,
soon returned the hammers and saws and
children's toys
And, to the house's delight, they brought two little
    boys.
As the parents worked night and day,
the children played and played and played.
And the house felt so much joy
for the man loved his wife and his two little boys.

First the man replaced the windows and doors
and put on a brand new roof.
And as if the house needed any more proof
of the family's love,
the man climbed a ladder high above
and replaced the broken gingerbread.
Then he said,
"Next I'll do the chimney,
and then I'll replace the siding."

So the man worked without,
while his wife worked within
over a mountain of books deciding
on carpets and paper and the colors of trim,
occasionally shouting a question to him,
"Can you buy a new brush when you go to the store?"
Or …
"What would you think if I tiled this floor?"
And most of all the house loved to hear her say,
"Oh, darling, I love this place more each day."
And the house felt so much joy …
again.

Within the house's heart
the woman worked her tasty art
of baking breads and cakes to eat.
And making meals and taking treats
to those who (the house supposed)
could not afford their own.
And oh, the sweet aromas seeping through its frame

filled the house with warmth and love.
And the house gave back the same.
Everyone who came said,
"It feels so peaceful hear.
What a lovely place."
As for the little boys,
often the house would hear them say,
"Dad, can you play with us?
Please?"
And the man would get upon his knees,
and his boys would run through the hall
and give him a shove
and over they'd fall
a big ball of giggling love.

Oftentimes through the day
the house would feel the couple pray
deep within its heart.
Prayers so warm like morning's glimmering.
Prayers so sweet like hot apples simmering on the
      stove.
And soon the house began to believe
that surely this family would never leave.

So you can imagine the house's surprise
at seeing tears in the children's eyes,
and hearing the man speak of a city far away.
And then he heard the older boy say,
"Dad, do you mean we're moving?"

Later large trucks drove up the street,
and ruddy men with muddy feet
walked through
and up the stairs,
moving out beds, dressers, chairs,
tables, books, and toys.
And when the trucks had pulled away,
the house heard the father say,
"Boys, come join your mom and me."

And then the house could not hear
so softly did the father speak,
but tears were rolling down their cheeks
as the family said good-bye.
And as the car pulled away
the house could hear the young boys say,
"Good-bye, wonderful home.
Good-bye, beautiful place."

And though the house was only wood
and could not wave good-bye,
and though the house could not embrace
the family now and cry,
still the family understood.

You see, for so long the house had stood
disgraced in disrepair.
Ashamed to show its crooked lines
Ashamed to shed the rotten vines
that hid it from the world.

But now, it seemed,
the house had been redeemed.
For love had changed it all.
That day,
all day long it rained and rained.
and the house felt so much love
And so much pain
until … a tiny car pulled in the drive
and out climbed a man and his wife.

As the sun broke through a cloud,
the house heard the man say aloud,
"Honey, won't this be the grandest place to
raise these little twins?"
And with her hand upon her belly,
with his arm around her waist,
the woman sighed,
"What a wonderful house,
What a beautiful place."

And just then,
sunlight smiled on the house's face
… again.

CHAPTER 9

Counting the Blinks

It's been an exciting year for championships in Lower Mundane. If your only source of news is the high school paper, you might find this surprising, since the varsity football team went from a cumulative 27 and 0 in the previous three years, to a winless season last fall. The varsity girls' basketball team won but four of their twenty-two games, and the boys only improved on the girls' record by three victories. So team spirit has been running a bit low over on North School Street.

However, back in January the middle school held an assembly to honor sixth-grader Eric Lloyd, who won third prize in the National Pass, Punt, and Kick Contest. Eric and his parents received an all-expenses-paid trip to Honolulu for the competition, which took place during halftime at the Pro Bowl. As his grandfather Pete Mundy loves to tell, Eric caught a gust of wind on his final punt. Unfortunately the gust was blowing the wrong way, or he might have won the whole thing. But Lower Mundane was pretty pleased with third place. Eric is a classmate of my son Lars, who says it couldn't have happened to a nicer kid.

Over at the lower school, second-grader Olivia Edgren went clear to the state Spelling Bee championship, and it came down to a contest between her and a girl from Cedarspring. They went at it for quite a while before Olivia finally missed on the word *separate*. As one might guess, she spelled it "sep-er-ate," which I've done a few times myself. When interviewed in the *Reporter Argus*, Olivia said she should have remembered there was " a rat" in that word. Her teacher predicted Olivia would be back next year.

And … last weekend at the state university, going undefeated in her age and weight class, Janine Care (Pastor Ryan's wife) won the divisional karate championship. No one was surprised, though some were unenthusiastic.

Ryan had invited our family to ride with him to Janine's competition and made plans to pick us up in his van at 10:30. This gave me time to perform a beloved Saturday morning ritual, driving our garbage to the town dump. I ran into Ryan there. He was sorting his month's worth of tin and glass into the appropriate bins.

"Morning, Pastor," I said, causing him to roll his eyes heavenward like he always does when I call him "pastor." I'm probably the only person who can get him to do so simply by using his proper title. This is probably because I've become his best friend.

A couple of days after the Cares moved here, Judy and I dropped by the parsonage to welcome them to town. I happened to mention to Ryan that if there was ever anything we could do to encourage them, they shouldn't hesitate to ask. So he didn't.

"Well," he said to me, "there is one thing, I've noticed that you and your boys enjoy shooting hoops in your driveway. Do you mind if my son and I join you sometime?"

So nearly every muggy evening last summer we played ball under the halogen glare of the streetlamps, sweating through our clothes and nurturing our friendship.

"Well, Pastor," I said, sky-hooking a coffee can into the bin, "today's the big day."

"Yep, this is it. Janine was pretty nervous when she left this morning."

"And," I said with a smile, "tonight's the big night, huh?"

"What do you mean by that?"

"You know what I mean." With a milk jug between my hands, I threw a head fake and released a perfect jumper toward the pile of plastics. "Tonight's the night you bring home a champion."

Slam-blocking the jug into the cardboard bin, he raised his hands in victory. "Well, yeah, but hey, I'm used to that."

Climbing back into my car I said, "See you soon, buddy."

"Actually," he shouted, "I'll probably be a few minutes late. I just got a call from Katherine Worthy, and she seemed upset, said Pross discovered the problem with our books and needs to see me this morning. So I'm going to buzz over there now, and then I'll pick you up on my way back through town."

Our treasurer, Prosper Worthy, has been a pillar of the Old White Church for nearly forty-five years. He and Ryan had been working closely together, trying to clear up a bookkeeping anomaly that had plagued the church during the four years since the fund-raiser for electronic bells. Two hundred dollars was unaccounted for.

Most churches simply would have written off the money long ago, but this accounting error (or whatever it was) led to whispered accusations against the church secretary, Lisa Martins. As a result, eventually the Martins and two other families left the church. The loss of three families is devastating to any small body, but especially so to ours, whose attendance over the Fourth of July dipped to single digits.

This was the splintered family Ryan found when he candidated here. If it had not been for the warm spirited counsel of Pross Worthy, he probably wouldn't have considered accepting the call at all. Pross had been a great encouragement to Ryan through this struggle and several others as well, most notably the Hallelujah Chorus Debacle and the Karate Club.

The Cares had hardly unloaded their moving van when they were thrown into the middle of a brewing musical controversy. Several young families, who had grown disillusioned with the Megatabernacle, left that congregation and joined ours. This was fine with the regulars, though none of them had ever expressed a particular interest in having new folks around.

Everything went smoothly for a few months until several of the new members began to complain about the "stodgy old church music" and the lack of praise choruses.

"Well, Pastor," the old members asked, "where do you stand here? Are we supposed to let new people come in and toss a hundred years of tradition right out the stained glass window?"

"Well, Pastor," the new members asked, "where do you stand here? We're not trying to ban the hymns and choir anthems. We just think all of us could benefit from a time of praise singing."

So Ryan did what he had learned to do so well in seminary. He appointed a committee to study the matter further. The committee in turn invited someone from the denominational headquarters to present a Saturday workshop followed by a potluck supper and a "Sing" to present a new praise-song hymnal supplement. It took a heavy sell to get the old members involved, but thirty of us attended, and it turned out to be a great day. It was great, that is, right up until the closing.

Ryan had just finished his benediction with, "And all God's people said Amen," when one of the new members asked if they couldn't close by singing together the "Alleluia" chorus. Several other new members oohed and aahed their approval. Ryan looked at them in disbelief but quickly recovered and, not wishing to alienate anyone, said he thought that would be a fine way to end a wonderful day of music.

What followed turned out to be a classic example of misunderstanding. What the woman suggested and what Ryan thought she suggested were two different things. The woman wanted them to sing the "Alleluia" praise chorus, which consists of prayerfully singing the word "alleluia" eight times in about as many notes.

Ryan thought the woman meant "The Hallelujah Chorus" by George Frederic Handel, which consists of singing "hallelujah" seventy-six times and many other words as well, using more notes than the total of those contained in the entire "Songs of Praise" hymnal supplement.

Ryan knew instinctively this was not a good idea, but he was determined to cause no greater division. If they wanted "The Hallelujah Chorus," then "The Hallelujah Chorus" they would have. He led off with his high tenor: "Hallelujah! Hallelujah!"

Amazingly, people stood up and joined right in, particularly the older members who recognized this as one of *their* tunes.

About thirty seconds later, it became apparent they had begun too high. The sopranos screeched, stretching their heads ever higher like baby starlings, large blue blood vessels bulging on their necks, faces twisting in pain. It didn't sound good.

Still Ryan would not give up. If anything, he was more determined than when he began. This hadn't been *his* idea! It was not *his* fault, but he knew the song, and they were going to finish what they had begun.

In the end, his will was not enough, however. They made it through the equivalent of four pages to the slow section, which begins. "The Kingdom of this world is become ..." That's where things really fell apart. Everyone stopped and stared at Ryan as he sang the next few lines all by himself.

"... the Kingdom of our Lord, and of his Christ, and of his Christ; and he shall reign for ever and ever. And he shall—"

"Pastor?"

It was the lady who had had this great idea. She was stifling a laugh. Actually, we all were.

"Pastor? I'm sorry, but I meant the other 'Alleluia' chorus."

I've learned that it's not too funny to bring this episode up often. Occasionally though, when Ryan beats me in "one on one," I'll wait until he's in his car and then say seriously, "Pastor, before you go, couldn't we just take a quiet moment to sing 'The Hallelujah Chorus'?" I sing at the top of my lungs until he has driven out of sight.

Several weeks later the Cares found themselves in the middle of another controversy when Janine posted an announcement on the bulletin board expressing her willingness to start a karate class if there was enough interest. The announcement took people by surprise, as Janine was the last person they would expect to be an expert in karate, a sport no one really understood. Janine had appeared to them the perfect pastor's wife, petite, polite, and plenty musical, leading the children's choir and playing the piano. They thought she was everything they had wanted, and now this!

Initial response indicated that the word *karate* was on the same spiritual level as astrology or maybe adultery. Again, unfortunately, the older members struggled the most, and Ma Bell spread their dissent as only she can do.

"Imagine a pastor's wife teaching karate!" Dorothea Dahl whispered disgustedly. "And get this, she'd love to teach right in the fellowship hall. Why, you'd never have caught Adell Swan teaching karate!"

Well, it was a bit hard to argue that point since the late Reverend Emil Swan's wife, Adell, was eighty-four when they left the pastorate, and she had been in a wheelchair for the better part of thirty years.

Ryan felt in this case there was no reason to form a committee. He understood the problem, and he faced it head on. Janine ended up getting her class, though not in the fellowship hall. She teaches at the grade school gym three nights a week. She has fourteen students, ranging in age from four to seventy, and twelve of them are Catholic.

Ryan has scheduled an appointment to speak with Dorothea Dahl, who now wonders aloud, and often, why the pastor's wife spends three nights a week with people from St. Theresa's.

"After all," she complains, "they're not the ones providing a parsonage."

No, it's not been an easy three years of ministry for Ryan. So Judy and I were not entirely surprised when we climbed into his van about an hour later than we had expected and heard him say sadly, "Well, here we go again."

"Oh, no," Judy said. "Bad news?"

"Worse than that," he answered. As we drove toward the university, Ryan told us the story.

"When I arrived at Pross and Katherine's, she met me at the back door. It was clear she'd been crying for a long time. Her face was distorted the way you only see in weeks following a funeral, and I figured I might be missing Janine's competition altogether.

"Pross came in the kitchen looking about ten years older than he did on Wednesday evening. I don't think he's slept much since then. I didn't know what was going on and really didn't know how to respond, but I figured Pross had found the accounting problem, and I suspected it was not a bookkeeping mistake. I figured it was a thief, one of those who had left so puffed up with pride. That's the only thing that would upset Pross so much.

"He pulled out a kitchen chair and said, 'Have a seat, Pastor,' which sounded odd because Pross is probably the only old guy in the church who calls me Ryan.

"I said, 'So it was a thief?'

"He said, 'Yeah Ryan, I found him,' and he handed me an envelope. Then resting both elbows on the table he hid his eyes in his hands.

"It was his resignation! His resignation as church treasurer and an apology for all the pain he'd caused the church over the last four years.

"I can hardly believe it. Pross Worthy stole the money.

"He says he never intended to do it. He swears that he's never stolen anything in his life, not even a candy bar, not even a lousy newspaper. And then he steals two hundred dollars from the bells fund. Says he was just fantasizing, playing some accounting games, and suddenly he had two hundred bucks in his savings. Says he never meant to keep it, but then the secretary realized that the money was missing, and he couldn't figure out how to give it back.

"I'm telling you guys, you've never seen anything so sad in your life. Old distinguished Pross was weeping his eyes out while Katherine cradled him like a big retarded child. Apparently Katherine never knew a thing. She's in shock.

"He says he's given the money back many times over, doubled his giving four years ago. Says he wanted to die when people started accusing Lisa Martins. Says he tried to leave the church, but then things had spun out of control.

"He's broken apart. He spoke to me hidden behind his hands. 'Pastor, I'll pay back any amount the church decides, I'll sell our cottage if necessary. It doesn't matter.' And then he looked me right in the eyes, anguish ripping his face. 'Ryan, if I need to leave the church, that's okay too. But please forgive me.'

"I did my best to assure him that our people will still love him, that there is always forgiveness. I hope I told him the truth.

"I was in shock myself, praying that I would say the right words when I didn't know what they were. As I was leaving I said, 'Pross, I really don't understand how this could have happened.'

"He said, 'Ryan, I swear to you, I never saw it coming. I was completely blindsided. Please, please forgive me.'"

We drove for a few minutes without speaking, our children sensing that silence was safest. Finally Ryan Jr., upset by his father's sadness, said, "Are you sure he did it, Dad? I don't think Pross could have done that."

"I'm sure, son."

Our spirits were lightened considerably at the competition, partly because of the excitement of karate but mostly because Janine was brilliant. At thirty-seven she is a little wisp of a woman, shorter than many of those in the twelve and under category. She, however, refuses to use the word *short*, referring to herself as "vertically challenged."

Whatever one calls it, she was easily the smallest competitor in the adult division. But she dominated, losing not a single round, rarely even receiving contact from her opponent. Even when facing a barrage of kick spins and thrusts, she seemed to know where the next blow was coming from even as it was being thought. She was a champion.

Afterward, Janine held her trophy for the news cameras and then headed down to the locker room to change. We waited, and the younger boys tussled on the mats.

Forty minutes later we ordered our food at Chi Chi's. At a table across the room, our children giggled and snapped their plastic straws. We relived some of Janine's finer moments until she said, "Oh, Ryan, what did you find out at the Worthy's?"

Ryan told the story again, and this time it was Judy who said, "It's hard to imagine how this could happen to him."

With the same quickness she had displayed all afternoon, Janine responded. "Sounds to me like someone was counting his blinks."

Ryan acted as if he had heard a revelation. "Of course! That explains it perfectly."

It explained nothing to me, so I said, "I don't get what you mean, Janine."

"Well," she said, "the problem seems clear to me. While preparing for this competition, I spent several days at the university with a master instructor who has coached national champions. I hadn't been challenged very much in competition and was beginning to feel insecure, realizing I didn't know my own weaknesses.

"One day, facing off across the mat, he said, 'Janine, I'm going to kick you above your left eye.'

"I took my defensive position, determined that I'd be ready for him. But strangely he didn't attack. He just kept talking to me slowly, softly.

"'You're good, Janine. Real good, but I know where you're weak. I'm going to bring my right foot up and touch right above your left eye. It won't hurt. Are you ready, Janine? Are you ready?'

"Well, let me tell you, I was never so ready for anything!

"'Here it comes, Janine.' He spoke so softly. 'Here it comes.' And that's all I remember."

She took a sip of coffee as Judy and I waited on the edge of our seats, leaning across the table. She took another sip and smiled.

"Come on, Janine, what do you mean that's all you remember?" I blurted out. "What happened?"

Ryan was beginning to enjoy this. "You know what, darling? I don't think you should tell him just yet. Maybe he should finish his lima beans first."

"Okay, Pastor," I shouted mockingly, "you know what I think? I think maybe this would be a good time for the whole restaurant to sing 'The Hallelujah Chorus.' What do you say, Reverend?"

"Like I was saying, Janine," he deadpanned, "hurry up and finish your story."

"Well, I wasn't sure what happened at the time," she said. "All I knew was that he had very gently kicked me in the head with a kick that, had he wanted it to, could have knocked me cold. Then he put his foot back down on the ground. And I never saw him move. I never saw the foot leave the floor."

She and Ryan were laughing at my mouth, which was hanging toward my plate of tacos. "So," I said, "please explain to me how this is possible."

"Remember he said he knew my weakness?"

"Yeah, yeah, go on!"

"Well, he did. The whole time he was patiently talking to me, he was also counting my blinks, finding a rhythm, anticipating the next and then, *wham*! I closed my eyes. It was only a blink, but I shut them all the way, and at the same instant, he kicked me in the head.

"That's one of the reasons I won my championship so easily today. He taught me how to compete without blinking. I can see where the attacks are coming from now."

"Do you get it?" Ryan asked. "I thought Pross was the most godly man I'd ever met. I never knew what his weakness was, but someone did. A powerful opponent was waiting patiently, counting the blinks. Pross used the word 'blindsided,' said he never saw it coming. I believe him."

We sat quietly for along moment. I stared into my coffee cup, contemplating Ryan's words.

Judy broke the silence. "I think you're right, you guys. And I think this whole ordeal is a great opportunity for the enemy to set up some others too, to kick them right where their pride is, right where their self-righteousness and bitterness are. He's counting our blinks even now. Sounds to me as though the church desperately needs some teaching from the master instructor."

The waitress came and took our plates as her fellow servers on the other side of the restaurant sang a poor Mexican rendition of "Happy Birthday" to some embarrassed patron.

We sat quietly.

Finally Ryan spoke. "I know now what has to happen tomorrow morning. Pross wants to share a short confession before my sermon, and I think he should have that opportunity. That's when everyone will have their guard down. They'll be ready to see Pross as a hypocrite instead of a repentant brother. Instead of embracing, they'll want to attack. For some, to choose the way of grace will be too difficult. Easier to choose a lawyer.

"So, Janine, as soon as Pross is done, I'm going to pull your big trophy out from beneath the pulpit and talk about what it means for each of *them* to be a champion now. It's time they face up to some of their weaknesses. It's time, right now, they learn about karate."

CHAPTER 10

I *Wonder*

It was our first Christmas here in Lower Mundane, Judy was in the kitchen on a snowy Advent afternoon, sorting a large pile of holiday mail. Christmas cards and personal correspondence went on the kitchen counter, flyers from Meacham's Hardware and Supervalue Drug were tossed in the garbage can under the sink. I had just come in the back door, my arms full of sweet white oak for the fireplace. The smell of cardamom bread awakened my senses to the season.

"Hey, Bob," Judy called, "listen to this." Holding a card, she read me an Advent poem. I don't recall all of it, but the poem ended with the phrase, "She held the one who for so long held her."

For days afterward I couldn't get the thought out of my mind. It transformed my Christmas experience. In that phrase lay for me the mystery of the Incarnation, the magnificent entering the mundane, God becoming man. The wonder of a woman carrying in her swollen womb the Creator of the universe. The wonder of a young girl giving birth to a baby who is its own father. The wonder of gently suckling a helpless thing without whom all life ceases to exist. Amazing? Wondrous? Awesome? Yes, and completely nuts!

Being raised in the church, I'd often thought about God's Incarnation as if it was expected. "Of course he became man. What else could he do?"

Then my wife says, "Hey, Bob, listen to this." The fuse is lit. With a flash my imagination ignites. I begin to wonder what this must have really been like for Jesus.

I wonder. Was he able to experience his birth? I mean, *really* experience it. Most of us have no conscious or perhaps even unconscious recollections of birth, and since he was totally human, he may not have either. On the other hand, since he was also totally God, he might have experienced it fully.

To suddenly feel the water drain from around him. To start to sense the panic, the involuntary need to breathe. *Oh, Father, maybe this whole thing was a mistake. Got to get out*!

And then *vooooshhh*!

Pressure!

Pain!

Falling!

Cold air!

The astonishing squawk of his own voice.

The warmth of the girl's body.

Oh, yes, there she is. She looks so much bigger from this perspective. How wonderful to be in her arms! And to rest. So tired … so tired … so tired …

Was he surprised to feel his mouth instinctively sucking as she helped him find his first meal?

When he awakened, did he recognize the callused hands of the carpenter? Gazing through blurred vision, did he think, *Oh, Joseph, I made you a very good man. Thank you for your faith.*

Did he know who he was even then? Some would say no, but I wonder.

How could God in any form not know who he was, unless of course that was part of the deal when he first spoke the idea of becoming man. Did he decide not to let himself know until the time was right? I wonder.

I wonder what God was like as a toddler.

"Joseph! Joseph! Come here quickly!"

At the sound of his wife's voice, the carpenter dropped his plane. He shot out the door of his shop and across the small courtyard to the house, wiping curled cedar shavings from his arms and leaping over white caps of scattering chickens. "Mary, what is it?"

Running through the door, he saw his wife sitting back on her knees, radiant and smiling like the young girl he had fallen in love with.

"Daddy," she said, speaking for her child, "I have something special to show you."

Beside her, standing for the first time, was their little boy, Jesus. One moment his face expressed a smile of satisfaction, the next a "whoa, I think I'm going down!" look of fear.

The big carpenter slowly knelt down by his wife and spoke in his most tender voice. "Why, Jesus, what a big boy! Are you standing up all by yourself?" Then reaching toward the child he asked, "Can you walk to me?"

With a shriek of laughter and a thump on the floor, the little boy dropped onto his bottom, rolled over on his tummy, and up on chubby knees. Then he crawled into the big man's hands. This was the little toddler who was God, not quite ready to take his first steps.

Then God said, "Let the land produce vegetation; seed-bearing plants and trees on the land that bear fruit with seed in it, according to their various kinds." And it was so....And God saw that it was good. (Genesis 1:11-12)

Yes, but that was God the Father speaking. What about God the Son? I wonder if he felt some things that he made weren't quite as good as others. I wonder if he ever ate dirt or put a bug in his mouth. I've never known a child who didn't.

I wonder if he loved cool, crisp, raw carrots, peeled by his mom and handed to him dripping wet. But if she took that very same carrot, diced it up and boiled it over a flame, the faint aroma may have triggered a gag response in the back of his throat. I wonder if God was surprised to find he just couldn't swallow this "good thing"?

Can you imagine Jesus as a two-year-old, his left arm wrapped around Mary's leg, his right hand reaching toward the table? If only he could get *one* grape, but his mother either didn't understand or simply chose not to give him one. Oh, she tried to give him everything else.

"Do you want your dreidel?" she says, spinning it on the floor. "How about this spoon? No? How about this fig? Do you want some milk?"

And then her child begins to scream, which clearly (at least clearly to *him*) meant, "I want a grape! Just one, silly little grape. I'm looking right at it! Can't you understand me?"

Desperate now, his mother says, "How about a little piece of lettuce?"

And then her boy has had enough. Throwing himself facedown on the floor, bumping his forehead in the process, God bursts into the tears of a tantrum.

I wonder if it happened.

Do you think as a little boy he was ever bored? Do you think he ever whined, "Mom, there's nothing to do"? Probably not. I'll bet there was always too much to do, and even if, like all boys, he did lie in the deep grass gazing into the blue, I'll bet he was never bored. Even if he did dangle his feet in the cool water on the occasional lazy summer afternoon, I can't imagine him being bored. Boredom is a choice I don't believe Jesus would make.

I wonder if as a young boy he ever used his power to heal, maybe without letting anybody know. As a seven-year-old, did he ever chase a wounded bird across the dusty street? Did he hold it in his hands, feel the trembling cease, and then, grinning, toss it in the air and watch it fly away?

Joseph could sense it coming, and this time very fast. It always began this way. A tiny white spot in his vision that grew brighter and brighter, eventually erupting into a flashing pain. This time it was coming fast. If only Eleazar the tanner would leave.

"Well, once again, Joseph," Eleazar nearly shouted in his booming voice, "thank you. Sarah is going to love this chair. And I don't believe she knows a thing about it!"

The spot was becoming brighter.

"Thank you so much!" The big man's voice was beginning to sound distant.

The last time Joseph had had one of these headaches, Mary and his eldest son were at the marketplace. His younger boy, James, had found him slumped over the table unable to move.

Now the tanner was gone. At least Joseph couldn't see him, so bright was the pain.

Joseph spoke, "Eleazar?" The strangeness of his voice startled him. "On your way out, could you please ask Jesus to come here?" Then Joseph lay his head in his own arms.

Moments later he heard his eldest boy's voice, "Father, I'm here."

Joseph always marveled that Jesus' voice never sounded distant. It was always clear, as if Jesus was speaking from inside Joseph's ear. And he never had to tell Jesus that it was the headache again. Even the fist time, when Jesus was just a little boy, he didn't have to tell him.

"It's okay, Father. It's okay."

The fear always seemed to drain from his body when Jesus spoke. Once Joseph mumbled, "Son, are you doing this? Are *you* making the fear go away?"

But before Jesus could answer Joseph had fallen asleep, and then there was just peace and warmth.

The Lord does not look at the things man looks at.
Man looks at the outward appearance,
but the Lord looks at the heart. (1 Samuel 16:7)

Yes, but this was God the Father speaking. Did God the Son always feel the same?

Did he never look at his skinny, preadolescent body and wonder when it would begin to change?

Did he wish he could grow up strong to look like Zadok, the brick-maker's son down the street?

Did he wish his beard would hurry up and fill in?

Did he ever long for young girls to look at him as they did some of the other boys?

Did he ever feel embarrassed by the persistent caravan stories about his absence, about being found with the old men in the temple?

When he went to the market with his mom and little sister, did small groups he hardly knew look at him from a distance?

Did he know they were talking about him?

"That's the carpenter's kid over there," whispered an older, tough-looking boy, pretending not to notice Jesus.

"Where?" shouted a fat kid with a bad complexion. "I don't see him."

"Shh! Will you please speak softly? He's *right there*!"

The boy pointed toward the woman holding a tiny baby.

Right behind her, trying to keep his little sister's hands out of a basket of figs, was the young Jesus, Joseph's son.

"Are you kidding?" asked the fat boy. "No way! That skinny kid? *He's* the one that they had to go back for?"

"Yeah, he's the one they found teaching the old men in the temple."

"Amazing!" The fat boy laughed loud enough that Jesus heard the voice halfway across the plaza. "He doesn't look too smart to me."

"Will you be quiet?" said another kid, shoving the boy in the back. "Do all you Galileans have to shout everything you say?"

"He's right," said the leader. "I don't think he looks too bright either. I'd like to find out if the child rabbi can fight as well as he preaches."

Lifting his screaming little sister high on his hip, Jesus noticed the boys leaning against the gate. With dread he realized he would have to walk past them. It seemed every week there were a couple more of them.

Then he saw the fat boy. Jesus knew him immediately, although they had never met. Jesus knew he wasn't from town. He was a fisherman's son, visiting from Galilee.

"Come on, Zach, give me a mango," the fat boy shouted, playfully trying to reach into the bag held high above his cousin's head.

"I thought you didn't eat them," teased Zach through a mango he held in his front teeth. He pushed the fat boy away with one arm, holding the bag with the other. "I thought you were on an all-fish diet."

"Okay, fine," shouted the fat boy. "I'll eat yours." With a swift move that surprised everyone, the boy grabbed the fruit from his cousin's mouth as though he were swiping a fly out of midair and shoved it whole into his own mouth. Choking back waves of laughter, mango juice running down his chin, he hid behind the other boys, holding them like unwilling human shields against his cousin's attack.

Watching from a distance Jesus smiled. Oh, how he wanted to get to know this boy! How he wanted to teach him and to be his friend. But that would have to wait many years.

"Come along, son," Mary said, lifting the produce.

Carrying his little sister, Jesus walked toward the gate, staying behind his mother a short distance so she would be through the gauntlet of stares by the time the boys spoke their threats. He knew if she heard them, their words would hurt her.

When Mary had passed, one of the boys said, "Hey, Rabbi Boy, anything you'd like to teach us today?"

"Yeah," shouted another, "tell us, how does God feel about children conceived out of wedlock?"

"Yeah, Rabbi," shouted the fat kid, joining in the fun, "my uncle says you're nothing but a little—"

Just then Jesus raised his face and looked right into the boy's eyes. It was not an angry glare. It wasn't even sad. It was a look of disappointment. But, like wine down the boy's windpipe, it stopped him mid-sentence.

Though he could not know it then, many years later this young fisherman from Galilee would see Jesus' eloquent glance again. Then too it would fill his eyes with tears. Then too it would fill his heart with shame. The boy turned away, unable to speak.

Three more steps and Jesus was out the gate and on the path to his home. In the distance he heard the tall boy mercilessly berating his cousin. "What's the matter with you, Simon, huh? Come on, Simon, you big baby, you better tell me why you're acting so weird. Come on, Simon, what are you bawling about?"

I know it probably didn't happen, but I wonder.

Did he ever trip over his own feet?
Did he ever blush in embarrassment?
Did he ever feel inadequate?
Did he ever laugh until he cried?
Was he ever afraid of the dark?
Did he ever feel homesick?
Did he ever dream about heaven?
Did he ever have nightmares about the cross?

Did anyone ever have to teach him *anything*? You and I learn from our mistakes, through trial and error. What about Jesus? I know he didn't sin, but did he ever make a mistake? Did he ever misquote Scripture? It's hard to imagine God misquoting himself.

I wonder if he ever hit a stone with a stick and imagined "The Babe."

I wonder, when he gazed at the moon if he ever, just for a moment, thought of Neil Armstrong?

I wonder if he ever wished he could have a frozen yogurt? I know this seems silly, but think about it. Is there such a thing as an anachronism for a timeless God?

"Well, you wonder way too much," some would say. "There's plenty you can learn about Jesus in Scripture. There's plenty written right out on the page for you that you don't have to wonder about."

Maybe. But I look at it differently. I think Scripture tells me all I need to know about Jesus, and it doesn't tell me a lot more than I need to wonder about.

"She held the one who for so long held her."
Isn't that magnificent?

CHAPTER 11

Pewdom, Peppermints, and Prayers

When I was a boy, at least once a year I would hop in the car with my folks and drive twenty-five miles over the state border to Dave's Showers of Blessings Religious Books and Gifts, the only store of its kind anywhere in the area.

Perhaps the most distinguishing characteristics of "Dave's" was its location. The store wasn't downtown with all the other shopping centers. It was in Dave's living room, where you could buy just about everything you could imagine to keep you and your entire church family pretty well blessed. Bibles (both King James and the radical new Revised Standard), flannel graph supplies, decoupaged plaques, communion cups, Scripture lamp shades, needlepoint bookmarkers, and inspirational recordings like "Brad Swanson and His Singing Organ" were all available at Dave's special religious rates.

Dave's slogan was "You find a better price in town, and we'll refund the difference." He seemed like an honest guy, and I believe he would have carried through on his guarantee had there been another Christian bookstore in town or maybe in the surrounding six counties.

Well, times have changed. The other day my son Lars and I took a ride back into the city and dropped by Good Tidings Christian Bookstore. Dave could have put most of his house in the music section alone. It's hard to believe so much is available to help my family in our Christian pilgrimage. Before us were resources for Sunday school, children's church, vacation Bible school, and after-school programs. Much of it was available on audio and video-cassette or compact disc, and there were rooms of written materials like songbooks, magazines, comics, board games, and collector cards.

"Just like baseball cards?" I said in disbelief. "Lars, come over here and look at this. Bible character collector cards!"

"Aw neat, Dad!" my boy said, grabbing the pack from my hands. "Let's see."

The cards were packaged so we could only view the front of the top card and the back of the bottom one. The top one was Simon Peter's rookie card and showed him sitting in a boat with a smile on his face as he gutted a big bass. The bottom one showed a very short list of the stats for Balak son of Zippor.

"Bible baseball cards," I said, honestly intrigued. "What do you suppose they'll think of next?"

"Probably this, Dad," Lars said, handing me a book. "It's okay to try it because it's a demo."

In my hand I held a colorful children's Bible entitled *The Revised Olfactory Version* or ROV. The subtitle invited me to smell my way through the Bible. I flipped to the gospel of John, where I was offered the opportunity to scratch the purple urn at the wedding in Cana and smell the wine. I tried it and several others as well. The wine, probably intentionally, smelled more like jelly, but the fish were remarkably realistic. So much so that I decided to pass on the pigs of the Gerasenes, though Lars gave them a scratch.

"Kind of like bacon bits," he said, wrinkling up his nose.

I left the store with several fine books, two CD recordings, and an idea. As far as I could tell, no one has yet written instructions for the implementation and maintenance of the most edifying church program I have ever experienced.

Maybe I should be the one to put it on the page, I thought. Maybe what most helped me as a child could help other children as well.

To introduce you to this program that I call "Pewdom, Peppermints, and Prayers," let me first offer a little history. Through most of my boyhood years, Helmer Larson was one of the older men in my little hometown church. He may have been the oldest; I couldn't know for certain, and it would have been rude to seek any sort of verification.

Helmer always sat in the third pew from the back on the right-hand side of the sanctuary. There was of course more room in the pew, and four or five other people usually filled it, but still the pew was Helmer's.

Other pews "belonged" to other people. Even with the church empty as my mother and I went down to vacuum on Saturday mornings, I could still identify each pew by name.

"This is Astrid and Arvid's," I would say to my mom. "And this one is Alfred and Grace's," and I could do so through the entire sanctuary.

I am describing for you a sanctuarial organizational system that we children called "Pewdom." The system operates quite naturally in almost every church in the country, but it is often improperly managed and occasionally blamed for some feelings of alienation among new families.

Let me describe for you how the system properly functions. Each pew is identified by the person or persons who have spent the most time in that pew. Thus the pew Helmer sat in was designated "Helmer's Pew," since he had sat in it for probably fifty years. My grandparents also had a pew of their own, as well as the Hallstroms, Olsons, and Bakers. Though my own parents had been in the church for fifteen years as a couple, and though my mother had been born, baptized, confirmed, and married there, they were still young people in their early thirties and thus ineligible for a pew of their own.

Pewdom was not something people talked about. It was just understood. I knew better than to ever sit in someone else's pew. If a visitor to the church did so, the "Pewie" was usually gracious, understanding that the offense was not intentional. However, if I violated the system and sat in the wrong pew, I committed an offense along the magnitude of someone outside the priestly order entering into the Holy of Holies.

That my family did not have a pew of our own had certain advantages. We could sit in any of the undesignated pews. I then had an additional choice, depending on congregational attendance—whether I would sit with my parents or my grandparents. Between the two of them I was usually guaranteed a seat with either one row in front of, or one row behind, Helmer Larson.

This was always a difficult decision. If I sat behind Helmer, the service was more exciting in a visual sense. Helmer had enormous old man ears, with an ample display of capillaries coursing just beneath the skin of the slightly discolored, shiny rims. But more remarkably and equally entertaining were the hairs that grew straight out of the ear canal, reminding me of some of my grandmother's thickly sprouting potted houseplants. I enjoyed sitting *behind* Helmer a great deal.

On the other hand, if I sat in *front* of Helmer, the service held a more exciting sensory promise. If I began to squirm even the slightest bit (as I always made a point to do), I would feel a big hand on my shoulder. Without looking back, I would reach into the old hand and remove a neatly wrapped red and white peppermint candy, which if sucked carefully would last me through the sermon, the closing prayer, and the benediction. Helmer Larson was one of the main reasons I mostly looked forward to going to church every Sunday morning.

I would like to recommend that we recognize Pewdom, which has functioned so beautifully in most of our congregations. Why not work in harmony with this natural process that is as old as the first wooden benches? Why not place families with young children near the old folks, who we know are going to be right where they belong every Sunday morning? Why not supply the Pewies with pockets full of peppermints and encourage them to meet the children who are squirming in front of them or peering into their ears from behind? Why not encourage these elders to send a birthday card, or go to a ball game, or maybe even take the child out for an ice cream cone? And most importantly, why not encourage each elder to pray continually for the spiritual maturation of his or her special little friend? I always knew Helmer was doing so for me.

I believe this program could help to usher many people into the family of faith. I also think it is a marketable idea, but I'm going to give it to you absolutely free. After all, I didn't create Pewdom. You did.

CHAPTER 12

The Rescue of the Yellow Finches

Rose Serillo lives at River Bend Manor. The name brings to mind a large estate with gracious old shady oak and shimmering willow, or perhaps lemonade and parasols on hot summer days. Indeed there was once such a place, but it burned to the ground early in the century, and now only old-timers Rosie Serillo and Winifred Rossi remember it. They remember the original manor well, because their father, Carmen Serillo, built it, and both women lived there as young girls. Besides these early memories and a strong family resemblance, they share little else.

Winifred was a gorgeous young girl, an early bloomer who at fourteen looked like Bette Davis. At eighteen she married a wealthy widower, Ross Rossi, who was thirty years her senior. Ross adored his young beauty and bought her everything, including most of Lower Mundane and eventually even her father's estate. The details of this transaction may be known only to Rosie and Winifred, but it is widely understood that the Serillos and the Rossis never spoke to each other again. Ross then died at fifty-three, leaving Winifred everything, including two spoiled children, Ross Jr. and Russel. Winifred held onto her wealth with white knuckles and to this day considers herself the queen of Lower Mundane.

Last summer Winifred called the editor of the town paper and told him she wanted a front page article about the convalescent home she was donating to the community, *and* she told him she wanted a reporter and two cameras at the groundbreaking in forty-five minutes. As a result, two reporters and three photographers were at the old River Bend Manor ruins, snapping away, when Winifred's limo arrived. Even so, Winifred was not smiling. Winifred never smiles.

Rosie has not smiled a lot in recent years either, though for very different reasons. She has survived mostly on public assistance for the last fifty of her ninety-six years. Early photographs at the historical society indicate that, if anything, she was even more beautiful than her younger sister. She too was engaged to be married but tragically lost her fiancé to the flu of 1923.

For two decades following, many men sought Rosie's hand, but she never again considered marriage. During that same time, her father lost most of his fortune and River Bend Manor. He lost the majority of it to his son-in-law, and then he took his own life. The paper reported a hunting accident, but today every junior high school student has heard the rumored truth.

Unlike her little sister, Rosie suffered greatly. She watched Winifred get richer and richer. She saw her sister take trips on yachts to tropical islands while she froze in Lower Mundane. Needless to say, Winifred was a constant emotional irritant.

At least once a month, the paper published flattering pictures of Winifred on the arm of a handsome man, strolling in Paris, sailing in the Mediterranean, sightseeing in Morocco. All of this was designed to impress everyone in Lower Mundane but particularly Rosie, whom Winifred no longer acknowledged. At times, it was just too much for Rosie, and she succumbed to long episodes of spiraling depression—unable to get out of bed, talking to no one but her two beloved yellow parakeets.

It was rumored around town that the only reason Winifred was donating the new River Bend Manor was so she could move Rosie out of the tiny apartment above the drugstore and get her into a place where someone would care for her. Winifred's friends spoke of this as a loving gesture, while her detractors recognized it as an attempt to appease her guilt for years of inexplicable torment and neglect. Either way, most people agreed it would be best for Rosie to move into the facility.

So she did, and it almost killed her. Of course any change at ninety-six is difficult, but it wasn't the move that caused her such pain. It was the regulation. There were only four rules for the new tenants, and the last insisted "Absolutely no pets." The director clarified for Rosie that, yes, that rule also included birds. So her two yellow parakeets were taken from her and donated to a very happy kindergarten class. Then Rosie, nearly catatonic with depression, entered her apartment at the new River Bend Manor.

It was here Judy and I met her.

Last November Judy noticed in the paper that the GoldenAgers and the Chamber of Commerce were looking for volunteers to deliver Thanksgiving dinners to needy families and individuals.

"You know, Bob," she said, "this might be a wonderful way for our family to serve someone. Who knows, it might even end up being a new family tradition."

I thought it was a wonderful idea. The paper announced a meeting for all interested volunteers at the GoldenAgers Hall on the Saturday before Thanksgiving. There we gathered with fourteen others, comprising ten driving units. As it turned out, this was perfect, because ten deliveries were on the list.

The GoldenAgers' president introduced himself to us since we were the only ones he didn't know. "The name's Bjorndahl," he said, grabbing my hand heartily and then giving Judy a hug.

This gesture would have seemed far more threatening and inappropriate had he not seemed so grandfatherly and nearly dead from too many years.

Judy said, "Very nice to meet you, Mr. Bjorndahl."

To which he responded, "Well, now, no need to be so formal, young lady. If I'd wanted you to call me Mr. Bjorndahl, I'd have told you that was my name, now wouldn't I?"

"Well, yes," I said, "I suppose that's true. What would you like us to call you, sir?"

"I told you, the name's Bjorndahl," he said, motioning toward some empty seats on a lime green sofa, "and this meeting is about to begin."

We sat down, and I chuckled, imagining Judy calling this old guy Bjorndahl without also saying Mister. I would probably stumble on that one a few times myself.

Bjornahl, whom everyone else called Art, then asked if anyone had particular folks they wanted to deliver to. About half did, and he was happy to oblige. This left seven of us who awaited our assignments.

"Okey-dokey," he said, adjusting his reading glasses and studying the crumpled list he held in his hands, "Who wants Rosie Serillo?"

He paused for a moment, staring at us over the top of his wire frames. No one volunteered, though in our case it was just because, not knowing anyone ourselves, we wanted others to have the first opportunity.

"Okay," he said, returning to his list, "that's what I figured. I'll come back to her. Let's move on. How about Francis Morelli?"

"Oh, I'll take Franny," someone said excitedly.

"Good. Now how about Chester Woods?"

"That'd be fine," someone else mumbled.

Down the list he went, one after the other, until Bjorndahl looked at us and said, "Sorry, young folks, but you're the only ones left, so you get Rosie."

"Rosie, it is," Judy said brightly. "What can you tell us about her that might help our visit to be special?"

"Well," he said, handing us a town map and shaking his head from side to side, "I can tell you plenty, but I don't think any of it will make your visit very special."

He then proceeded to share Rosie's story, which I have already related, and a number of other stories probably none of us should have heard.

"If I were you, I'd just go in, unwrap her meal, maybe tell her to have a nice day, and then leave," he said, "If you stay, she's just going to start cryin' like she has for the last forty years, tellin' you how she can't go on another day, cryin' 'bout how she's got no one who cares for her and how no one loves her. It's really pitiful, and if anyone can ruin your Thanksgiving spirit, believe me, it's Rosie Serillo."

As we left, I must admit, I felt a little threatened by the prospect of this lamentable lady, and I expressed my concern to Judy. But she was undaunted.

"Well, we'll make her awful day a little less bad then, won't we?" she insisted.

On Thanksgiving morning we picked up the meals in the GoldenAgers' kitchen at eleven o'clock. Besides the foil-covered food, Judy brought a quilted warming pad to carry it in, and each of the boys held a small houseplant wrapped in bright yellow bows.

While we drove down toward the river, I told the boys that if Miss Serillo seemed very sad and weepy, it was just because she was old and not really in touch anymore. They could have handled the whole story, but there wasn't really time, nor did it seem necessary.

We headed north on River Road and drove into the circular parking lot at the new River Bend Manor. For a prefabricated building, it was quite lovely. We found Rosie Serillo's small efficiency apartment just past a nurses' office on the first wing.

"Here we go," I said apprehensively and rang the doorbell.

From within, I heard an audible response, which I took to mean, "Come in."

But Judy held my arm and whispered, "Wait, just a minute."

Soon the door opened nearly halfway, and we saw smiling at us the most beautiful old woman I have ever seen. She was small, but much stronger than I'd expected from Bjorndahl's description. In fact, stronger than Bjorndahl, and her eyes were positively sparkling, joyous! Her long white hair was wound neatly on top of her head. Her clothes were clean, and her apartment smelled like fresh apple pie.

I thought we had certainly knocked on the wrong door and was about to apologize, when Judy said, "You must be Rosie."

"And you," she said with a sweet smile, holding out both arms in greeting, "must be the Strombergs."

We stayed about half an hour, which was long enough for Judy to warm up Rosie's meal in the microwave and heat up a cup of tea. Rosie praised the small azaleas over and over and found a place for them on her kitchen windowsill. She asked the boys about school and how they liked their new house, and they talked to her as easily as they might have a great-grandparent. When we left, Rosie gave *us* the apple pie.

"Oh dear, I hope it's okay," she fussed. "I've not made a pie in many years."

Later, after our own turkey meal, I ate two pieces. It was delicious.

That was the first of many pleasant visits to Rosie Serillo. "Rosie, may I ask you a personal question?" I inquired one day. "We always look forward to our visits, but the first time we came here ..." I proceeded carefully.

"Well, frankly, we were pretty nervous. We'd been warned that you would be a very sad person."

I expected her to say something like, "Well that's because you talk to Art Bjorndahl too much." But she didn't.

Instead she took my hand and said, "I *was* a very sad person. Most of my life I was depressed and sad, always afraid that no one would care for me in my old age, always convinced that no one loved me. But then God talked to me and everything changed."

She definitely had my interest. "Rosie, do you think you could explain to me what you mean when you say God talked to you?"

Rosie smiled. "When I came to live here, I was in worse shape than I'd ever been. I'd been depressed many times, but nothing compared to this, and it was all because of my birds."

"Oh yes," Judy sympathized, "we heard about your parakeets."

"My two yellow parakeets," she said. "All the years I lived by myself, I had my parakeets. Of course from time to time I'd lose one or the other, but I always replaced them with another nearly the same. Always yellow. They were my babies. I loved their sweet music every morning. I loved their sunshine color. They were the brightest things in my dark life.

"When I moved here, I was told I couldn't bring them with me. I was never given a reason. I was just told that birds weren't allowed. Of course I've always suspected that it was just Winnie's way of saying she was still in control of my life."

For a moment I saw a flash of anger in her eyes but nearly as quickly they softened again, and she said, "It didn't really matter about my sister. What mattered to me was that my birds were gone. I know it sounds awful, but I didn't think I could survive without them. Truly, I wanted to die.

"Then one day I walked out on my tiny patio and, lo and behold, I saw a yellow finch building a nest in my eaves trough. As I watched her fly back and forth with tiny bits of lint and twig, I felt my heart starting to beat a little bit faster.

"For weeks I watched the finch and her mate. I was still not well, but I began to feel better. Then I noticed they were bringing tiny worms to the nest, and even though I'm ninety-six years old, I could hear the sound of the babies crying out for food. It was wonderful! Then, just as quickly as my joy was returned, it was again swept away.

"One day it rained very hard. I saw the nest when it turned over, and I watched the female and probably all the babies wash right down my gutter spout and under-ground. For a couple of days the male returned and sat on the edge of the gutter, and he would try to sing, but it was just so sad.

"That's when I thought I was going crazy, because I could still hear the mother and the chicks crying. For several days I couldn't get the sound out of my head, all the time crying. And I just lay there on the couch. Too sad to cry myself, I just lay there. Even in the night, inside my head, I heard the little birds.

"Then one afternoon, lying right there on the couch, I heard a voice say, 'Rosie, look in the drain basin.' Well, I looked around to see who it was. I thought maybe it was one of the maintenance boys, but no one was there. Then I heard it again, 'Rosie, look in the drain basin.'

"Well, I didn't even know what a drain basin was, but I started looking out there around the patio and, sure enough, in the grass out by the fence there's a steel cover about the size of a big pie plate. Then again I heard the voice say, 'That's it, Rosie, now look inside.'

"So I got down on my hands and knees, because you know when you get old like me you can't bend down anymore, and I lifted the cover off the basin."

Rosie's eyes were filling with tears, and for a moment she fumbled with her handkerchief, unable to speak. "The basin was almost filled, but right above the water line there was a little edge, and on that ledge ..." She wiped her eyes, smiling through her tears. "Earthworms had been washed up. And beside them sat the yellow finch and her three little babies, dry as could be. They were all alive!

"I reached down, and one by one they jumped up on my finger and then hopped out onto the lawn. I watched them fly into the tree. And then I sat on the grass for a long time listening to their music. Then I remembered how Jesus had told me about the basin and—"

"Wait a minute, Rosie," I interrupted. "Did you say it was Jesus?"

"Yes, I remembered how he had told me about the basin so I—"

"Rosie, how did you know it was Jesus?"

"Well, I didn't know the first time, but then I sat there and I remembered the voice. And just as I did I heard it again. I didn't imagine it! I heard it, just as real as could be, and it said, 'Rosie, do you understand now?'

"Then I waited, and again he asked, 'Rosie, do you understand?'"

"Well, I didn't understand, and I said so aloud. When I spoke, my own voice didn't even sound as real as his. Then I waited, and he said, 'Rosie, if I care for these little birds, don't you think I'll care even more for you?'"

Judy reached out and held Rosie's silky hand. "And that's when you knew, Rosie? Is that when you knew it was Jesus?"

"Oh, no," Rosie said with a sigh, "After he told me how much he cared for me, I sat for quite a while longer, listening to the birds and marveling at what had happened. Then I crawled over to that little garden bench, because I couldn't get up, and that's when he spoke again. His voice was even more beautiful than before, and I realized that I had already begun to miss hearing it.

"'Rosie,' he said, 'I will *always love you.*'"

Rosie reached out her other hand and held mine. "That's when I knew, Bob. When he said, 'I will always love you,' that's when I knew it was Jesus."

The three of us sat in silence for a moment gazing out the patio slider. A sliver of sunlight split the clouds and lit the gracious face of Rosie Serillo. This was the old woman whom people had avoided for fifty years, the old woman Bjorndahl told us would steal our Thanksgiving spirit. Her face shone with the youthful essence of God's joy and peace. She had been touched by the magnificent.

We go often to see Rosie, not so much to bless but to be blessed ourselves. In her late years, she is making up for lost time and experiencing life in abundance, abundance of laughter, abundance of prayer, abundance of thanksgiving, *and* abundance of birds.

Last week, we counted fourteen finches in her backyard.

CHAPTER 13

Where Did These Kids Come From?

The longer I live with my children, the more I understand that they do not belong to me. Make no mistake, Judy and I are their biological parents, but we do not own our sons, and we did not make them either.

God allowed us to participate in a small way and to that extent we are responsible for them being here, but I did not fertilize an egg and Judy did not grow a child within her womb. We are not that creative.

Judy did not even have her babies. If anything, her babies had *her* until they'd had enough, and then they came out—not when we wanted them to, by the way. They came out when their Creator said it was time.

I will always remember the thrill of holding these tiny strangers in my hands, wondering who they would become. Their personalities had barely begun to form, their features still vaguely undefined.

Together we gazed at each of these miracles and wondered, "Oh, God, did we make this beautiful child? Did he actually come from us?"

And God lovingly answered, "Why, no, where did you get that idea?"

Of course we didn't hear him. If we had been so perceptive, I might have responded, "What do you mean, where did I get that idea? Just look at him, God! He looks just like the Hawkinson side of the family."

Or, "What do you mean, God? You know he's the perfect image of my own mother."

I don't think this would have bothered God a bit. He knew all along that if we didn't know it then, we would learn later that they were not ours. Our boys have just been entrusted to our love and care for a short while.

I'm also learning that it is not our job to determine whom they will be. That has been taken care of too. To be sure, we do have great power to influence for good or bad, but we can never improve on the children God created for us to love. From fine genetic dust he wove a sinew through our lineage, pouring marrow of spiritual mystery and breathing into each child marvelous gifts that no microscope can detect.

Can science explain our son Nathan, who has drawn beautiful pictures since he was old enough to hold a big Crayola in his chubby hands?

From the beginning Judy told me, "Bob, look at what this child is drawing. I'm telling you, this is a gift!"

Well, at the time I wasn't so sure. Maybe all toddlers could draw like that. Maybe all two-year-olds could hold a Magic Marker and connect the tiny flowers on our new sofa. I hadn't looked closely at other families' furnishings to compare.

Now that the child is fourteen, and astounding many outside our family with his natural ability, I realize that Judy was right. It *is* a gift, and it would be no less a gift if we could trace his talent to some artistic Viking misfit who painted Danish seascapes when he was supposed to be pillaging. It is still pure mystery.

Nathan's talent did not go unrecognized by his little brother, who even as a toddler couldn't understand why he didn't draw as well.

"It's nowt fayo," he would pout.

"What's not fair, Larsy?"

"It's nowt fayo, dat I can't dwah pwetty yike Nate."

We explained to him many times that we loved his pictures just as much as we did his brother's.

"But his ow beddo!"

"Well, maybe," we'd comfort, "but Nathan's older, and he's practiced a lot longer, and God made him with a very special talent for drawing. But Lars, God made you with very, very special talents too."

"What ow day?"

"Well, we don't know yet. But what God gives is always very special, and boy, is it going to be fun to find out what he has for you!" What we told him was true.

As this little boy grew, we began to notice that God had given him a spiritual sensitivity that could not be explained by genes. I remember tucking him into bed one night when he was five years old.

After prayers he said, "Dad, tell me about Easter again."

As simply as I could, I told him the story, explaining how much God loves us all and wants to live in our hearts.

When I was done, in a sweet, trembling voice, he said, "Dad, I want to ask Jesus to live in my heart too."

In the primary grades we noticed Lars was concerned about his little friends. He was happy when they were happy and sad when they were sad. He was often the first to say, "Dad, I think we need to pray about something." Or, "Mom, I can pray for your backache, if you want me to."

This sensitivity is certainly not what Lars would have picked. If given the choice, he would have chosen the spiritual gift of dribbling. Though he is becoming a fine basketball player, his success as an athlete, just like his dad's, will come as a result of much hard work. This year in sixth grade, all his buddies made the middle school traveling basketball team. Lars was cut.

As the only one cut, quite naturally he became the outsider. He could no longer define himself as "one of the guys." Of course he was upset.

Two weeks later, as Judy and I sat next to him at bedtime, he prayed and again validated his gift. "Dear God," he said with a smile on his face, "thank you so much that *all* my friends can start their first day of basketball practice tomorrow. I'm so excited for them, God, and I pray that you will help them to play well and to get better and better every day. In Jesus' name, Amen."

Judy and I stared at each other in disbelief. Truly, he did not come from us. Nor did his brother. Their gifts have a mark of magnificence that we cannot claim as our own. We can but delight in "our" sons and ponder, "Where did these kids come from?"

CHAPTER 14

Henny's Last Haircut

Both our boys were born with flowing locks Absalom, the handsome son of King David, would have died for. Nathan's hair begins halfway up his forehead, thick and straight, layered in a half dozen shades of radiant amber. On a gusty day it streams like Adam's across the ceiling of the Sistine Chapel, before surrendering softly back into place.

Lars prefers to comb his coarser auburn mane straight back in waves that look like sculptured red oak and cherry wood buffed to a resplendent satin sheen, like a young Viking explorer.

I remember as a young parent hearing a child psychologist suggest it was not only harmful to criticize but also to praise children for things for which they were not responsible. It is better to criticize poor behavior than a poor attribute. Better to praise great accomplishments than great traits.

If our children do experience any latent damage as a result of our inept parenting, it will be because we err on the side of unmerited praise. My response to the psychologist would be, "Hey, buster, it wasn't all our fault, okay? You just don't see hair like theirs every day!"

Everywhere we took the children, they were lavished with unmerited approval. It was usually women—women in the bank, women in the grocery store aisles, and especially women at the beauty salon.

"Oh, my word! Will you look! What I wouldn't do for a head of hair like that."

When we lived in the city, all four of us had our hair cut at Ada's Salon, often scheduling our appointments on the same afternoon. When we moved to Lower Mundane, we continued to drive back to Ada for the first few months, but as school activities began vying for time, I thought it might be more convenient for the boys and me to try Henny's Barber Shop. I'd been eager to do so anyway because the old red and white pole outside Henny's reminded me of my childhood.

As a little boy, every other Saturday morning, I went with my dad to Carlie's Barber Shop. We didn't make appointments in those days. We just arrived early or stuck our heads in the door. If there were too many waiting, we came back later.

While we sat in vinyl chairs listening to WFRM, I read *Boy's Life, Mechanics Illustrated*, Dell comics and any issues from a large assortment of professional wrestling publications. Another pile of thick, glossy magazines towards which I felt some curiosity were stacked under the coffee table, but my dad and I never looked at those.

After a long time, when I was beginning my squirming mode, Carlie would give me a nod, and I'd climb on his chair. From there I looked at myself in the mirror behind the tall blue translucent bottles of sterilized combs. Above me, Carlie worked on my head, whistling in a soft trill the way only old guys do. Behind him I could see all the others reading their magazines and waiting in line. I was in no hurry now. Everyone had to wait for *me*.

In those early years Carlie cut everyone's hair pretty much the same—short. When he was done, he pressed a button on his lotion machine and, through a wet, wheezing sound, filled his hand with hot, mint foam. With this he spread a warm lather evenly over the top of my ears and the back of my neck. Then, holding with one hand the end of a smooth cowhide belt, he flicked his jack-knifed razor in his other hand, exposing the shiny long rectangular blade. With deft wrist movement like a musical conductor, he ran the metal edge over the leather. "Shhhharp! Shhharp! Shhharp!" it warned.

"Don't move now," he added, and I sat stone still as he scraped a tickling line of definition around his work. Then my dad would give him seventy-five cents, and we would head home.

In later, longer-haired years, I went to Carlie's by myself after school, often fearing that my folks had called ahead with styling specifications that did not match my own. Still I enjoyed the atmosphere of his shop.

So it was with some nostalgia that I herded the boys into the car on a bright Saturday morning and headed for Henny's.

As a young man in the mid 1930s, Hennes Hogfelt bought the shop at the corner of Mundane and Main. He ran it successfully by himself until 1975, when his son-in-law

Lenny Burleson returned from barber school and began buying into the business. Lenny was still in his early twenties and became very popular with the younger men and boys, who had adopted longer styles and intuitively distrusted the aging Henny.

They were not unfair to do so. An old man with sharp scissors and a razor does wield some power, and apparently Henny occasionally crossed a line of sensitivity. With two or three masterfully quick strokes he could make a hippie look like a marine. The worst part was he seemed to enjoy it and certainly showed no remorse for his actions. Henny felt it was his right to cut hair as he always had.

Predictably, as Lenny's younger clients grew in number, Henny's got old and died. This put Lenny in the awkward position of having long lines waiting for his services while his father-in-law stood idly by his chair. Soon there was really no reason for Henny to come to work. Oh sure, he cut Pete Mundy's hair every couple of weeks, but Pete really didn't have any, so that was easy. Otherwise Henny just stood there looking pathetic.

Such was the scenario as we entered the shop. It was full. There was no place to sit, so the boys found a spot on the rug by the television and began to watch "American Gladiators." I greeted my buddy Eric Burt, who was the only person I knew, and then noticed Henny, now well into his eighties, standing feebly by his chair.

When our eyes met, his countenance brightened discernibly, and he said, "Well, hop right up here, young man, and we'll take care of you."

Every head lifted from behind the magazines to see what I would do. I was about to accept, pleased that I didn't have to wait, but Eric spoke on my behalf. "Henny, I think my friend here probably needs to have Lenny cut his hair."

There was a collective sigh as everyone seemed to relax a bit before returning to his reading. I was surprised to hear Eric speak so curtly, but I decided I ought to follow his lead.

"Thank you, sir." I said as kindly as I could, trying not to sound even remotely condescending. "I really appreciate it, but I'll wait."

I don't think I did a very good job, because the old man's lower lip began to quiver as he slumped dejectedly down in his chair. Being completely unprepared for this, I almost gave in and said, "Well, hey, why not. Give me a little trim."

But Eric, looking quickly my way, held out his hand as if to say, "No, no just let it be," and that was all I needed to understand the situation.

An hour and a half later we left the shop looking every bit as stylish as we had ever looked before, and we'd paid about half the money. We even all received a complimentary lemon sucker. It wasn't a big Tootsie Roll Pop like I used to get when I was a kid, but it was a nice, authentic touch. Though the wait was a bit long, it was no worse than driving forty minutes to Ada's Salon, and the boys agreed Henny's was more convenient. So from then on, Henny's it would be.

Several weeks later, Lars said, "Dad, can I get a bowl cut?"

"Well, son, that would probably depend on what a bowl cut is."

"Dad, it's so great! All the guys are getting them."

"Yes, well, that doesn't mean a whole lot to your old dad. So supposed you tell me what a bowl cut is, and then I'll tell you if you can have one."

"Well, Dad," he continued enthusiastically, having never anticipated that he would still have my ear so far into this conversation, "a bowl cut is where you comb your hair straight down in every direction and then your barber shaves your head with a razor, way up over your ears, and it looks as though he cut your hair with a bowl on top of your head. It's really cool, and I think you'd find it very attractive."

"Oh, I see what you mean," I said. "So you look kind of like Moe from the Three Stooges."

"Yeah, Dad, right," he said brightening steadily. "In fact, you look just like Moe."

"Well," I said, "now that I know what a bowl cut is, the answer is no, you can't have one."

He hesitated not even a second. "Well then, Dad, can I get a buzz cut?"

"No, your mom would not survive it."

"Then could I shave my initials on the back of my head?"

"No, I don't think so."

"How about your initials?"

"Lars, look at me," I said, trying hard not to sound too much like my own father. "You look great the way you are, son! Your mom and I have let you try some pretty cool things with your haircut, and besides, you have radical hair before you do anything. You don't have to try stranger and stranger things just to look like everybody else."

He gave up more quickly than I would have when I was his age.

"Yeah, okay, Dad," he said, not really very disappointed. "I figured that's what you'd say."

The three of us developed a routine. About once a month we went to Henny's and waited in line while watching "American Gladiators." This was usually fine except that Lars's hair grew faster than Nate's and mine. This disrupted our schedule when there was something special for which he needed to look particularly good. Such was the case last week.

He had landed a part in the school play and would be performing Thursday and Friday evenings. On Tuesday we realized, too late, that we should have planned a trip to Henny's the Saturday before. I would be in the city all Wednesday, so Tuesday evening I called Lenny at home and asked if he thought there would be a long wait if Judy dropped Lars off after school. She could then run some errands and pick him up afterward. Lenny assured me that the wait would not exceed an hour. This would enable Lars to get home a little after 4:30, relax for a few minutes, and grab a quick bite of supper before returning to school for his final dress rehearsal at six o'clock. It seemed like a viable plan.

I returned home Wednesday about five o'clock and found Lars sitting on a kitchen stool with a tablecloth tied around his neck, barber style. His eyes were puffy and his cheeks tear-stained. Judy was working over him with the trimmer on my electric razor, apparently providing the bowl cut he had said he wanted so badly.

On the top of his head all the wave was gone. Chunks of hair half an inch long stood straight out in random stalks while some long strands lay flat to his scalp like corn after a hailstorm. It was something like the haircut his brother Nathan had given him when he was a toddler.

"Well, Dad," Judy said sadly, speaking for Lars, "it's not been a very good hair day."

Before I could ask what had happened, the phone rang. It was Lenny. "Say, Bob, I'm calling to tell you how bad I feel about Lars. Believe me, I tried to fix it, but he insisted it was fine."

"Listen, Len, I came in the door only seconds ago and found Judy trying to fix the worst haircut I've seen since the Sex Pistols. Everyone's a little upset here. Maybe you could fill me in on the details."

"Well, sure, I'll try," he said apologetically. "Lars came in about a quarter to four. I told him to have a seat, and I'd be right with him because I was just about to finish up with Art Berdino. So Lars sat down and was reading a comic for a minute. Next thing I knew he was over talking to my father-in-law and telling him how he had always wanted to try one of his haircuts. I couldn't believe my ears. I turned around, and of course, Henny was beaming like he'd just won the lottery and was saying, 'Well then, hop right up here, young man, and I'll give you a haircut like you've never seen. Yes, sir!'"

As Lenny spoke, I watched my son, and I began to understand what had happened. "Well, Lenny, apparently your father-in-law is a man of his word. I know I can say honestly *I've* never seen anything quite like it."

Lenny continued. "Listen, Bob, I tried to talk Lars out of it. I told Henny I thought you'd want me to cut Lars's hair. Henny knows I'm the boss now. He was disappointed, but he was ready to hand Lars back over to me. But Lars said, 'No, I know my dad would want Henny to cut my hair. It's okay.' So now, you see, he really had me in a spot. It's not like Lars is a little kid. I didn't feel I had the right to force him to change chairs.

"Then Arn Westdahl came in and said he was in a hurry so I got busy on him. When I finally turned back, I realized Henny had made quite a mess. But Lars acted like everything was fine, just carrying on a conversation with Dad like they were old buddies. You need to know he was never in any danger. Dad hasn't used sharp-ended shears for several years now."

Judy, working carefully over one particularly deep furrow of cowlick, gave me a frustrated glance.

"Okay, Len," I said, "I don't think I understand the situation, and I realize it's not your fault. But I *do* wish that you would have cleaned his head up a bit."

"I was going to Bob, really! I didn't want to embarrass either one of them, so I meandered over and suggested I trim up a few little spots. But Lars wouldn't let me touch him, said he thought it looked really nice. In fact, he said it was perfect the way it was.

"So I sent your boy out the door looking like a POW. I really felt bad, called you just as quick as I could. I'm sorry."

"It's okay, Lenny," I said, still staring at my young service man. "It'll grow back."

"Oh, and one more thing, Bob. I can't remember when I've seen Hennes so happy. You know, the whole family's been trying to get him to retire for years, but he'd hear none of it. He's just been sitting in here day after day, hoping someone would want him. It's been a tough thing for all of us.

"Today when he finished with Lars, he said he was done. Wouldn't be in tomorrow. In fact, wouldn't be in any more. He said he's going to call Pete Mundy and see if he can ride with Pete on his delivery truck. Said he might be able to get Pete to take a couple of hours off and maybe do a little fishing. I can't believe it! He cut Lars's hair and then hobbled out of here with a smile on his face. And that's not all—he was whistling! Bob, I haven't heard him whistle in fifteen years."

I thanked him for calling and assured him we would all be back, though in Lars's case it might not need to be until sometime next school year.

"Well," Lenny said, "Dad didn't even think to charge him today. But whenever Lars comes back, his next cut is on the house too." We both laughed and said good-bye.

Judy was nearly done with the repairs. In reality Lars looked more like Curly than he did Moe but, with the exception of a few white nicks cut down to the scalp, it didn't look too bad. Standing back admiring her work, Judy said, "Well, what do you think? Shall I open up my own shop?"

"I'm sorry, Dad," Lars said, wiping the back of his neck, trying to shrug away the itch. "I just couldn't stand to see the old guy sitting there, no one paying any attention to him. It didn't seem right. I just couldn't stand it. Then when he was cutting, I knew he was doing a lousy job, and I was so worried about how I'd look for my play, but I couldn't hurt his feelings and let Lenny fix it."

"It's okay, Lars," Judy said. "You followed your heart and did the loving thing. That's a wonderful thing about you. But usually when you follow your heart, there's a price to pay. Still in the end, son, it's always the best thing for everyone."

"I don't know, Mom," he said, looking at his head's rounder reflection in the microwave oven. "I don't know how it's the best for me. I look pretty stupid. I can't believe I asked you guys if I could get a haircut like this."

"No, Lars," I said. "Your mom is right. You did the right thing, and we're proud of you—and now you're famous."

"What do you mean?"

"Well," I said, rubbing his bristly crown, "Hennes Hogfelt worked in that shop for more than fifty years, *you* were Henny's last haircut."

"Yeah, Dad," he said, starting to smile, "and judging by the looks of it, I think I did a great deed for the men of Lower Mundane."

✐ooters

I've noticed that changes, even small changes, come slowly in this town. But when they do come, they are often profoundly felt. Perhaps no recent change has had more effect on our community than the retirement of Roy and Mipsy Apple.

In 1952 the Apples bought an old service station out on Route 6. They renovated the building, adding a kitchen, a parking lot, and a beautifully hand-painted sign heralding "The Apple of My Eye" and, in smaller script beneath, "Fine Family dining." And so it was for thirty-five years.

Even before the construction of the airport, requiring the new four-lane connector, people used to drive thirty miles from the city to savor Roy and Mipsy's fine family cuisine at unbelievably low prices. The "Apple," as it became known, put Lower Mundane on the map.

In 1985, when the new Megatabernacle went up just a half mile down the road, they scheduled their Sunday morning worship to end at 11:30 solely so people could make it to the Apple before the other churches let out. This did nothing to endear the Megatab to most folks in town, who then had to wait about an hour while the "Megatabbers" porked out.

Roy and Mipsy worked hard and lived well enough but never became rich. People appreciated this because clearly, had the Apples desired, they could have charged much more, and people would still have come. They also could have added a bar like all the fine restaurants in the city. Roy and Mipsy knew these things too, but the restaurant was the joy of their life. They loved serving people, and that was more important to them than wealth.

Then in 1987 Roy had a mild stroke, and they made the wise decision to sell the business and settle back a bit. Several realtors in town inquired about handling the sale, but Roy didn't think it was necessary.

"Thanks anyway," he said, "we'll just put up a sign, and see what happens."

It didn't take long before they began the process of screening several interested buyers. One guy happened to mention over the phone that he would love to add a video arcade, and with a smile Roy erased his name from the list. Two others indicated they had discovered in their survey that the Apple was indeed outside the boundaries of Lower Mundane and thus could legally apply for a liquor permit. They too noticed that Roy became less prompt in returning their urgent phone messages. Then finally word spread around town that Roy and Mipsy had found their buyer.

His name was George Tudor, and he appeared to be all the Apples could want. He was in his early thirties, had worked in nearly every aspect of the food business since he was a teenager, and best of all, he was familiar with the

Apple. He called Roy from Chicago and mentioned that he and his wife had enjoyed dining there several times while driving through the town. His wife was from nearby Chastain, and the first time he visited the area he had vowed to live here someday and own a restaurant just like the Apple. He said he could fly in on Saturday, if that would be convenient, and then he would like to try a church in town before returning to Chicago on Sunday afternoon.

Mipsy said she knew George was the right buyer from the moment she looked out the kitchen window and saw the handsome young man crawling out of his rental car. Not only did he share their philosophy of service, but his personality was so attractive that by the time he left the restaurant two hours later he knew half the customers by name and several of them had shown him pictures of their kids.

George was not able to pay what Roy and Mipsy were asking. In fact, his offer was fifteen thousand dollars less than all the others, but he said it was absolutely all he could pay. They decided it was enough. He was the man they wanted in their restaurant. George told them they could reach him in Chicago anytime during the week, but on Saturday night Roy told Mipsy he didn't see any reason to wait.

"George said he's going to the Old White Church," he told her. "I'll just meet him in the parking lot after the service and tell him it's a deal."

So that's what he did, and everyone was happy... for a while.

My pastor, Ryan Care, remembers shaking the hand of the charismatic George Tudor on the first and last Sunday he ever graced the doors of the church. "I remembered thinking how sharp this guy was," Ryan told me. "You couldn't help feeling attracted to him. But, you know, it's interesting. Later Janine told me that he gave her the creeps."

Well, George Tudor left Chicago, but he didn't move to our town. Instead he bought a sprawling brick Georgian on the seventh green of the Meadowbrook Country Club. He didn't move with his family either. Apparently he had forgotten to mention to the Apples that he had been divorced twice and hadn't yet married the woman he lived with. After the closing papers were signed, George never spoke to the Apples.

Within a month, a bar was installed where Roy and Mipsy had served their smorgasbord every Sunday since Cokes were a nickel. Several walls were removed to make room for the dance floor, and a new neon sign reading "Tooters Bar and Grill" was installed on the roof.

Ryan said he originally thought that the name was just a takeoff on George's last name, Tudor. Then he stopped in one night to pick up a pizza and realized he had naively overlooked another connotation.

George had hired all new waitresses, and Cynda Moore was the only local girl who got a job. It was obvious to most that Cynda got the job not because she had ever waited a table in her life, which she hadn't, but because she had the same look as the city girls George had hired. Ryan said all the waitresses wore T-shirts tied high above the waist with "Tooters" written across the front.

"That wasn't so bad really," Ryan told me, "except the 'Os' in 'Tooters' were made to look like two big eyeballs. I had to work pretty hard to keep from staring back."

If anything, Tooters became even more successful than the Apple, though serving a different clientele. The parking lot was no longer filled with family station wagons and mini-vans. Now it was filled with detailed pick-ups, the kind with gun racks in the back window, driven by men who wore baseball caps or cowboy hats. I wondered where these guys were coming from, since I'd never seen a cowboy hat in Lower Mundane. Apparently George Tudor, counting his money in the back room, knew all along that when he put up his sign, these people would crawl out of their holes, thirsty for what he was serving.

Well, we all grieved the loss of the Apple and the intrusion of George Tudor. Of course none suffered more than Roy and Mipsy. Angry folks around town passed petitions and sought legal counsel, but George had covered all his bases. It looked as though Tooters was here to stay.

Ryan began to feel he ought to pay George a visit. "I really don't know why," he told me. "I just feel a kind of nudge in that direction and, if I've learned anything during my years of ministry, I've learned to trust the nudge."

George had signed an attendance card that one Sunday morning, and though he'd not requested a visit from the pastor, Ryan thought George should get one anyway. *And* it was probably best not to try to schedule an appointment. "You want to come along?" Ryan asked.

Saturday morning we pulled into Tooters a little before noon. George's new Saab was the only car in the lot. "I'll bet he's thrilled about that," Ryan said sarcastically, pointing at the car.

Someone had apparently sideswiped him, taking off the mirror and the trim along the driver's side.

"For our sakes, we'd better hope it didn't happen this morning," I said.

The front door to the restaurant was locked, and no one answered our raps, so we went around back and let ourselves in the kitchen. I felt a little nervous. If the front door was locked, then we probably weren't welcome. I felt the kitchen door was intended for people who worked there, and I said so, but Ryan felt that included him.

I *am* working here," he said, waving me on. There was no doubt: for Ryan this was a mission.

We passed through a swinging door and a short hallway that led by the darkened bandstand filled with amps and midi equipment. Each piece silently flashed tiny red lights as if to warn of our intrusion. I could see by the long banner that a country band named Tequila Stupor was providing music for the weekend.

From here we followed the sound of George cursing loudly at somebody over the phone. "So that's it?" he raged. "So you're telling me there's nothing you can do?" For a short moment there was silence, and then without a word he slammed the phone down on the receiver. That's when Ryan and I stuck our heads in the door. George didn't notice us. He sat behind the cluttered desk, moaning a desperate prayer, his face hidden in his hands, a cigarette smoldering between his fingers. "Oh, God, please," he groaned. "Please, God!"

I felt a little embarrassed, like maybe this would be a good time to tiptoe back out the way we came, but Ryan was following the Spirit now, nudge by nudge.

"George," Ryan said softly.

George bolted out of his chair as if God had answered his prayer in person. His cigarette flew against the wall. A cup of cold coffee poured over a pile of scattered papers, and George screamed, grabbing the Styrofoam cup with one hand and stomping frantically on the smoldering rug.

"How'd you get in here?" he demanded. "What do you want?"

If it had just been me, I would have answered both questions directly. I would have told him I came in through the kitchen, and all I wanted to do was leave unharmed, but this was not Ryan's response. Ryan was following the nudges.

"We came to pray with you, George," he said.

I looked at Ryan, and I'm sure my jaw dropped discernibly.

I didn't realize we had come to pray. I might not have come had Ryan asked if I'd like to go pray with George Tudor.

"Who told you?" George demanded, his neck throbbing red. "How'd you find out?"

Ryan was unshaken. "No one told us anything, George."

"Then why did you come here, now"" he demanded, leaning forward, glaring over his desk.

"I don't know, George," Ryan answered softly. "I just knew we had to come."

For a moment no one spoke, and then we watched as the flush left George's face and his body relaxed back down into his chair. Covering his face with both hands, he muttered so softly we could hardly hear, "What's there to pray about, Pastor?"

Ryan motioned to me, and we sat straddling two empty beer kegs. "George," Ryan said softly, "suppose *you* tell *us* what we need to pray about."

We waited a full minute in silence.

No one uttered a sound. George slumped in his chair, still covering his eyes. I glanced at Ryan, wondering if perhaps our "friend" had nodded off.

Then finally, without changing his posture, he muttered all on one note, "I've got what they call Retinitis Pigmentosa. I'm going blind, no cure. I can only see what's directly in front of me. It's like looking through a dark tube. I walked into that filing cabinet and ripped the skin off my ribs this morning. I tore the side off my car last night, because I couldn't see my own garage. It's getting worse every day."

We sat in silence again, and I prayed quietly, knowing Ryan was waiting for a nudge. Finally he spoke. "George, I'd like to pray for you."

George had not moved at all since he first slumped into the chair. Now he raised one little finger of consent.

Ryan's prayer was typically short and concise. "Dear God, you know this man. I ask that you would heal him inside and out. In Jesus' name, Amen"

Afterwards I asked George if there was anything we could do. He said no. We left him in his office, still behind the desk, exhausted and despairing. I would not see him again for six months.

The summer was the hottest in recent history, and Tooters was packed every night. Often when I drove by I thought of George and wondered how he was doing. Sometimes I prayed for him, though perhaps not as diligently as I ought to have. To be truthful, I didn't think there was much hope.

I have friends who have gone blind, or deaf, or suffered painful deaths after grueling illnesses, and *they* all loved God. It didn't seem likely to me that God would spare George Tudor. Why should he? Had I the power to heal, I'm not sure I would have chosen to use it either.

Nearly three months after our meeting with George, on a scorching late August afternoon, I was mowing the small remaining green left on my lawn when Ryan pulled his old station wagon into my driveway.

"Howdy, Pastor," I greeted him, killing the mower's din and wiping my sweaty face on the front of my T-shirt. "So what's the good news for today?"

"The good news for today is unbelievable!" he said, shaking his head. "Are you ready for this?"

"Why not?" I replied. "Go ahead! Let me have it."

"Well, I went down to Tooters today."

"Oh, did you get another nudge?" I teased. "Or did you just want to check out Charlotte Palomino and the Kentucky Studs?"

"Neither," he said with a laugh, "but I heard them rehearsing, and they were pretty hot. No, I got a call earlier this week from George asking if I could drop by."

I sat down in the shade as Ryan climbed out of the car and leaned against the front fender.

"So go on," I prodded, "what's the good news?"

"The good news…" he said with a sly smile, "…is that George Tudor is completely healed."

It took me a moment to take it in as I stared dumbly at Ryan.

"Yeah," he said, "that's the way I responded too. But he's healed. Has been for a week. Yesterday he got a clean bill of health from the doctors. They say they want to do some more tests, but he's completely cured. No one knows what to think about it."

"Well what about George?" I asked. "What's he think about it?"

"He doesn't *think* anything about it. He *knows* what happened. Last weekend, his girlfriend dropped him off at the bar a little before noon. He was sitting in his office feeling sorry for himself when a voice called his name. Of course he couldn't see much, but he heard the voice just a few feet away, and he knew that no one else was in the room. It scared him half to death. He literally couldn't move, just sat there with his heart pounding out of his chest."

"Wait a minute, Ryan. You don't suppose Rosie Serillo has been hanging around the bar lately, do you" I teased.

"No, I doubt it." He laughed. "But there are some definite similarities in their stories. The voice called out his name again, 'George, don't be afraid. This is Jesus, and I want you to go out in the parking lot. There you'll find a little puddle. Make some mud and rub it on your eyes.'

"George said he didn't feel in a position to argue, though he knew there wasn't a puddle in the parking lot. It hasn't rained since the first week in June, and he hasn't had a sprinkling permit since the Fourth of July. But the voice said to go outside, so he did, and that's where he found the tiny puddle. Really it was more like a damp spot in the dirt. He found out later it was where his girlfriend had spilled a full glass of iced tea.

"He bent down, worked the soil into a sandy paste, and rubbed it on his eyelids. Then he went back in, feeling a little embarrassed, hoping no one had seen him. He sat in his office for about two hours, waiting to hear the voice. He even worked up the nerve to say, 'So, what do I do now?' But Jesus didn't answer, so he just sat there until he fell asleep. He said it was the most wonderful sleep he's ever had.

"He didn't wake until the kitchen help arrived at three o'clock. Then he decided to wash off the mud since he thought he would look pretty stupid if they saw him with dirt all over his face. He went into his bathroom, rinsed his face in the sink, and when he looked up he could see perfectly.

"He was so excited he ran right in and told the kitchen help. When the bartender came in, he told her too. In fact, he told everyone who came to Tooters last Saturday night. He told them about the voice who said it was Jesus, about the puddle and the mud and the sleep. Of course everybody could see that he was healed.

"I think one of the cooks plays in the worship band out at the Megatab. He must have spread the word around the church because on Tuesday, Reverend Coates paid a visit to Tooters. He asked George if the rumors about his healing were indeed true, so George gladly told him the story. Apparently though, Reverend Coates was pretty tough on him, asked a lot of theological questions George couldn't answer, so George threw him out."

"Wait a minute, Ryan," I said. "Do you mean that George threw out The Reverend Dr. Harold Coates?"

"Well, not right away. He let him stay until Harold told him that the same Jesus who had healed him also wanted him to shut down Tooters. George said that Jesus hadn't mentioned anything about that to him.

"Coates sneered, 'So you think Jesus is just going to come out and talk to you every time he has something to say?'

"George explained that so far that's the way God had always done it, and until God told him to shut Tooters, he wasn't going to do it. So if Reverend Coates wanted to see him again, he could just drop by for happy hour.

"Then Coates blew up at George, saying he didn't think George had ever been blind because Jesus wouldn't heal a man who ran a pit of vipers like Tooters. That's when George threw him out and called me."

"Incredible!" I said.

"Yeah, and that's not all. I read George the story of the blind man in John 9, and he broke right down and cried like a baby. He'd never heard it before! Then the phone rang, and he got busy talking to some booking agency in Louisiana and had to excuse himself. He wants to get together next week though."

"Incredible!" I repeated.

"Yeah," Ryan responded, "no kidding!"

When Ryan left, I went right in the house and shared the story with Judy, nearly matching Ryan's enthusiasm.

With the passing of several months, though, something began to gnaw within me. A more spiritually mature person would surely praise God for his faithfulness, for answered prayer, and for the marvelous work done in George Tudor's life. But unfortunately that has not been my response. Instead I have struggled, identifying more strongly than I wish to admit with the pharisaical Reverend Harold Coates.

The truth is, just like Reverend Coates, I do not understand why God would heal a man like George. I understand that God doesn't need to check with me before he does anything, but now that he's done something for

George, I'd prefer if George would act a little more grateful.

What do I mean? Well, for starters it would be nice to see him make some sort of traditional evangelical public confession. *And* I too would love to see Tooters change its name to Tudor's and look more like the old Apple. But clearly that is not expected to happen. Travis Thunder and the Rainmakers packed the place out for three wild nights last weekend. Judy was driving home with both our boys and nearly hit some cowboy staggering out of the parking lot.

When Ryan drove in my driveway again last week, I told him, "Sorry, buddy, but all this business about George makes me mad. If God's going to come and talk right in his ear, which by the way, he's never done for you or me, *and* if he's going to heal George with a glass of iced tea spilled in the parking lot, then at least George ought to have the decency to change his life!"

Ryan was ready for me. "It sounds to me, Bob, like you're the prodigal son's older brother, aren't you? Your feelings are hurt because your dad's paying so much attention to that rotten kid. Doesn't seem fair, does it? What's your deviant brother ever done to deserve such love while you're the one who's always been so faithful? You've never turned your back on God, have you?"

"Ah, come on, Pastor," I countered, "you know that's not the story at all. It doesn't have anything to do with me. I'd be happy to recognize George as my brother, but he won't even admit to being part of our family. He refuses to live by any family rules. He's not the prodigal come home. He's still just the prodigal."

"Oh, so you think God made a mistake when he healed George?" Ryan asked sarcastically. "You think God didn't know what he was doing?"

"I don't know, Ryan," I blustered. "I don't know what God's doing."

"Well, I don't either," he said softly, "but that's nothing new. When I don't know what God's doing, that's a pretty good indication that he's doing something .God doesn't need you and me to set George straight. God can handle George all by himself, and he is. Have you heard that no one can get out of Tooters without hearing about George's eyes?"

"No," I said, "I guess I hadn't heard that."

"Well, it's true. He tells everybody. Have you heard that now he's treating all his employees like real people? Have you heard he's paying them on time and letting them keep all their tips?"

"No, Ryan," I said sheepishly, "I haven't heard anything."

"Well, it's true. And get this! Yesterday I saw Roy and Mipsy in the post office, and they told me they received a check in the mail for $10,000. It was from George. He promised them another $5,000 before the end of the year. He asked for their forgiveness. He said he could have paid them the full price all along, and he knows now that what he did was wrong. He didn't have to do that, but God's changing him, Bob. He's changing him from the inside out.

"The Apples are still torn up about Tooters. They asked me what I thought they should do. I told them I thought they should forgive him. I told them I thought we all should."

Ryan and I sat on the lawn for a while, and I pondered the things he had told me. Of course he was right. God does know what he's doing. I want George to become a Christian and act like the rest of us, but God has a more primary and perfect desire. God wants to make him into a new creature.

I sat with my pastor friend, humbled again, knowing that God desires to make me a new creature too, and he's had a lot longer to work on me. Of course George and I are not really that different. God reaches no deeper to George. Changes, even small changes, come slowly to both our hearts. But when they do, they are profoundly felt.

CHAPTER SIXTEEN

A Little Chunk
of Consequence

The doorbell rang about four o'clock today. It was Pete Mundy with a package. Pete retired from the U.S. Post Office six weeks ago, after carrying mail in this town for more than fifty years. The Veterans of Foreign Wars had a huge celebration for him out at the Legion Hall and gave him a wristwatch with a Pony Express rider etched on the face. The guys down at the post office also gave him a watch and a nice plaque that read "Neither rain, nor snow, nor dark of night shall keep me from my appointed duties, but a doughnut and a fresh cup of coffee is another matter altogether."

Pete had always been slow. I thought when he retired I might begin to see all my mail during the morning hours, and that has mostly happened. I say "mostly," because I do receive my letters and correspondence early, but my packages still come later in the day. This is because Pete couldn't handle retirement. No one was surprised.

At the beginning of the month he began a courier service of his own, Pete's Courier Business. I have no idea how he gets my packages, but he does. If they are sent UPS or U.S. mail, Pete brings them. If they are Federal Express, it's Pete at my door.

"Got a package for you here, and I'll be darned if I can guess what it is," he said, holding a small tube of brown paper, weighing it from one hand to the other. "It's pretty heavy though."

When I first moved here I might have insisted he hand it over, but I knew now that would be a waste of energy. "Come on in, Mr. Mundy," I said, opening the door and stepping aside. "Why don't we just find out what you have there. Cup of coffee?"

"Aw, well..." He checked both his new watches. "Yeah, sure, I have a minute. The package there? It's from your dad."

He was right. It was a thumb-sized piece of broken clay tile from a drainage pipe that my dad had sent me. Pete took one look and, realizing he had delivered nothing of great value, said, "You know, I probably ought to pass on that coffee after all. I'd hate to keep my other customers waiting." With that he left.

I stood in the kitchen and held the broken piece in my hand. There was a note with it from my dad. "I found this while cleaning out the cellar. I thought you might like it."

I ran my fingertips over the sharp, broken edge. It was very heavy for its size.

I was fourteen years old, and I didn't feel I needed to be reminded about lawn mower safety. I had been mowing our lawn and a few others for several summers, but each year my parents recited a long litany of lawn mower rules:

Be careful! Always stay alert. Never reach beneath the mower when the engine is running. Never use the mower close to other people, especially children. When mowing near the house or cars, always shoot the clippings in the opposite direction. Always look ahead for toys, stones, or anything that might be in the mower's way, and above all, never mow when the lawn is wet.

The last one seemed particularly important to my mom. She remembered hearing of a young boy, about my age, whose sneaker slipped on the slick grass while he pulled his dad's new rotary mower up a steep bank.

"Aw, come on, Mom, I'm not going to ruin my shoe," I would say, mockingly rolling my eyes.

"This is nothing to joke about, young man. Now you listen to what your dad and I are telling you, or you're going to end up hobbling around like that little boy, and who will be laughing then? Huh?"

Well, I wasn't sure. It almost sounded as though *she* would, which seemed unlikely.

The flying foot story had been far more effective several years before, when I had first heard it. I thought maybe Mom had just made it up to scare me. But then I told my buddy, and he said it was true. He had heard it in the Buffalo news. He said the kid's foot flew clear across the lawn and over a fence and landed in a neighbor's backyard. Then they couldn't find it because the neighbor's dog buried it.

I didn't even want to mow the lawn then. I didn't care about the $1.25 I could make. It wasn't worth cutting off my foot. But that was then, and now that I was fourteen, I knew better.

I knew I wasn't going to lose a foot. I hadn't even had a close call yet. Oh sure, I had dinged a few rocks, shot an old golf ball clear across the creek, and accidentally sprayed the side of our insurance man's Mercury Montclair with wet grass clippings. But I was still walking, and I'd not done any real damage. All the rules and warnings didn't seem necessary anymore.

So one late August, Saturday morning, with a final, "Yes, yes, okay. I understand!" I shot out the door to mow.

I think we as people have a difficult time grasping the concept of consequences. This shouldn't be surprising; there are many things we have difficulty grasping.

We're not very good with viruses, for example. You would think with all the billions of dollars that have been spent studying viruses we would have a pretty good idea what they are, how they work, and what we can do about them. But we don't. We can't seem to do a thing about the common cold. There's a fortune waiting for anyone who can find a cure, but no one's done it yet. And the same is true for many cancers, MS, lupus, and psoriasis. During their teen years, some present-day dermatologists dedicated their lives to finding a cure for acne, but their children are still poking at pimples just like their folks did.

There are many things we have a difficult time grasping, so it shouldn't be surprising the concept of consequences is one of them. But it is surprising.

Maybe it's because we're taught from the beginning of our lives about consequences. We experience them firsthand, and then, the next time we're confronted with a choice, we forget what we should have learned.

I used to tell my toddling children not to get too near the wood stove. "Hot! Hot!" I'd say, making my worst daddy scowl. But of course they had to touch the stove or a cup of coffee or a hot piece of pizza before they began to understand the concept of consequences, the idea that when you do something you shouldn't do, something unpleasant will happen to you or to someone else.

Fortunately, most children will not go through life repeatedly laying their cheeks on the griddle or licking the frozen flagpole. A couple of consequences are usually all it takes to change that behavior for good. But, that being true, I should think when I tell my toddler to stay away from the cellar stairs, right away the child should think, "Oh yeah, I remember yesterday when Dad said not to go too near the stove, but like an immature little crawler I did anyway, and boy, it was really unpleasant. Yep, I remember that like it was yesterday. And now Dad's making that same scowl, and so I think I better not go too near the stairs because they might be even more painful than the stove." Wouldn't you think this process would occur? Well, it doesn't. Not hardly ever.

Okay, maybe I'm expecting too much from a toddler. Maybe it should take a year or two before the child understands and takes my word for it when I say there will be a consequence to a particular action. But should it have to take well into the teen years or even longer? Can't they just trust my experience, alter their behavior, and avoid the pain? Apparently not.

The grass had gotten longer than my dad liked, but we had had two weeks of solid rain, which had prevented me from doing my job. Perhaps I could have gotten to it yesterday, but yesterday was also the first sunny day that we had had at the community pool. So I made the decision any fourteen-year-old would, to be with my buddies.

I recall telling my mom, "I'd sure like to do the lawn, but with all the rain we've had I'd hate to take a chance and mow it if it's still a little damp. But, if you think it's important, Mom, I'll go at it. I suppose I could wear my old leather dress shoes. They're quite a bit heavier than my canvas tennies, and they'd probably stop a blade if necessary."

Mom told me to go swimming.

That was yesterday. Today I yanked on the rope, and the old Briggs and Stratton fired on the fourth try. For an hour or so I nearly trotted behind the mower as it pulled itself and me over our lawn. My dad, working alongside, raked the grass into damp, fragrant piles of green.

Around the back corner of the house, for the last two weeks, water had been pouring continually off the roof and into an eaves trough. From there it flowed through a rusty downspout connected to a partially buried piece of red clay drainage tile, allowing the water to leach gently out onto our lawn.

My dad had always warned me about this spot. "If you hit the top of that tile, it's hard to tell what kind of damage you would do. You've got to be really careful there, son. Are you listening?"

Shoot, I'd mowed directly over it dozens of times, even with the blade at the lowest setting, and I hadn't nicked it yet. Today, having set the mower up to get through the thick lawn, it was even less of a concern.

What I couldn't see, beneath the high grass, was the erosion that had occurred from the heavy rains. Unknown to me, a small ditch now extended a few feet out from the mouth of the tile and five or six inches wide. When the mower wheel dropped into this trap, the blade hit the top of the tile with a deafening crack.

Thirty feet away, my dad had been reaching down to pick up another pile of grass for the wheelbarrow. He bolted upright as a fist-size chunk of tile, flying at blinding speed, stuck him in the chest.

I jerked away from the angry mower and instinctively turned to see my dad hitting the ground. He lay on his back, and he did not move.

We no longer have toddlers. Now we have teenagers and the concept of consequences is, if anything, more difficult than ever. My children don't fall down the stairs as much anymore, and they don't touch hot things, but they mow the lawn now, and swing golf clubs with their friends standing only inches behind them.

They laugh and say things like "It was so funny, Dad. Toby swung his nine iron, and it just barely missed the side of my head. It actually swiped my hair." Or they say more ominous things like "Dad do you realize I'll be able to have my driver's permit next year at this time?"

Our younger child recently videotaped our older more responsible child making a blowtorch by lighting the end of an aerosol paint can.

"We were just doing a little magic show thing, Dad," he protested. "We'll buy you some more paint, okay? It's no big deal."

"Look at the edge of the can, son. Would you please read that aloud for me?"

"Warning! Extremely flammable. Keep away from heat," he read, beginning to get the point.

"Please tell me, son. Is a flame hot, and if it's shooting out the nozzle, do you think that would be considered dangerously close?"

I'm sure he won't do that again, but what will be next?

Dad was only unconscious for a few seconds, and I was there when he came to and grabbed me, pulling me toward himself, fear distorting his face.

"Get down! Get down!" he rasped, disoriented, trying to find his wind.

"Oh, Dad," I said, trembling, "I hit the tile pipe. Dad, are you okay?"

Then, as he realized what had happened, the haze of confusion began to clear, and he lay back on the lawn and relaxed.

A few moments later, in the kitchen, my mom cleaned the wound, and I waited for the lecture. Finally she said, more calmly than I had expected, "Now do you understand?"

I nodded my head, and that was all that was spoken.

The jagged missile left some nasty lacerations and a deep purplish scar right where the collar bones meet. If it had struck even a fraction of an inch higher, it would have penetrated the soft windpipe.

I think we people have a difficult time grasping the concept of consequences. I've been living for some forty years now, and I still often don't get it. I've been seeking to follow God for most of that time. Still, every day he insists on reciting for me a long litany of safety rules: Be careful! Always resist evil. Always confess your sin and ask for my forgiveness. Never hold a grudge. Never judge a brother or a sister. Treat others exactly the way you would like them to treat you. Never worry about anything at all. Always make your request known to me… and the list goes on.

"You've got to be really careful here, son. Are you listening?"

Sometimes I wonder if it's necessary for God to be so persistent. After all, I'm still walking. And I haven't done any terrible damage yet. But what I can't see beneath the unkempt corners in my life is the erosion. Erosion is the enemy's weapon. "God," I protest, "I don't have to be careful about everything. You see, God, I've been over some of these areas a dozen times. I'm okay."

Then the wheel drops, and who knows what damage is done?

So God patiently recites again, "Be careful, always… never… and above all…"

But still I have a hard time grasping this concept of consequences. So sometimes it's helpful to pick up that shard of red tile pipe and hold it in my hand. I'm painfully aware that it could be an old photo of my father instead, the way I remember him when I was fourteen. I pray God will always be so merciful.

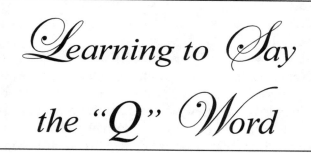

CHAPTER SEVENTEEN

New gardeners soon discover that
all seedlings are not alike.

Crocketts' "The Victory Garden"

Yesterday Judy and I went to our son's first freshman basketball game.

"Can you believe we're old enough to have a boy playing high school ball?" Judy said, proudly waving to our son, who was tripping through layup drills. "Maybe all your time in the driveway has finally paid off."

Basketball has been an important thing in our family. In our previous home, with the sloping driveway, I spent weeks tearing down an old horse shed in the backyard to make room for a ball court. It became the envy of every kid and quite a few dads in the neighborhood.

In our Lower Mundane home, I pestered my contractor about keeping thirty feet of driveway nearly flat from the garage doors to the box elder tree.

"I'm not sure I can promise you that," he warned. "The asphalt guys have certain codes for drainage, you know. I'm just not sure."

"Listen," I insisted, "I'm spending a lot of money here. I should think you could find a way to give me a few feet of flat blacktop."

Well, it worked. The weekend before the family moved in, I stayed up into the early morning hours digging a hole and mixing concrete so the hoop would be in place when the kids rode in the driveway. I even put a 500-watt quartz light on the side of the house. I wasn't trying to make great ball players out of my kids. I did it because we have such a good time playing basketball, pig, horse, lightning, varsity, kill your buddy, and many other variations of the sport. It's a game you can enjoy all your life, whether playing in leagues with full teams, one on one, two on two, or all by yourself.

Sitting in the gym with Judy, I had to admit it did seem incredible that our boy could be playing freshman ball.

That was yesterday.

Today our son came home from school and informed me that he wanted to quit.

"It's just not worth it, dad."

"What's not worth it?" I countered.

"It's too hard. I'm the worst guy. I'm never going to even get in."

Only a year or two ago I might have told him to forget about quitting. "You've made a commitment. Now you stick it out." Today this response didn't seem quite appropriate, though his rationales were unsound.

"Listen, Nate, even if you are the worst player, that's no reason to quit. And even if you don't play in the games, that doesn't mean you're not important to your team. Especially *your* team. There are only ten of you on the roster."

He sat across the kitchen table from me, a scowling stone, staring hard somewhere over my head. I'd seen this posture before. I'd seen it years ago when I'd asked, "Didn't I tell you not to eat the Popsicles on the new carpet?" I'd seen it when I'd asked, "Didn't I tell you not to hit stones with the baseball bat?" I'd seen it when I'd asked, "Didn't' I tell you this would happen if you left your tennis racket behind the Toyota?"

He stared. I waited.

"Besides, Dad, my grades aren't too good. I think practice is taking away from my studies."

"Nice try, son, but your grades weren't too hot before. In fact, you're probably using your time better now than before the season began."

A year or two ago this might have been the end of the discussion. I would have said, "Do you understand, son?" and he would have mumbled something and sulked a little bit. Later there might have been a passing complaint, but that would have ended it.

Today my teenage boy stared at the wall, and I waited.

I was not surprised to find us in this posture. I'd seen it coming in a number of comments over the last few weeks.

"So, Nate, how was your first day of practice?" I'd asked excitedly.

"Exhausting, I've never been so tired in my life!" he had said, flopping facedown on the sofa.

"Hey, that's good. A couple of weeks more, and you'll get into shape and feel great!"

But he didn't. A few days later he had complained about late practices. "I can't do it, dad. I'm not getting home from school till eight o'clock."

"Sure you can do it," I'd boosted him. "Hang in there. You'll be fine."

But he wasn't.

Today, he stared. I waited.

"Okay! Look, Dad, I know how disappointed you are."

There was a touch of anger now as he rolled his eyes. "I know you'd be happier if I was some kind of superstar. But I'm just not! Okay?"

He expected this to escalate the argument, but since we both knew I held no such expectations, there was no reason for me to attack back.

I said calmly, "You know I don't care that you don't want to play ball. I just don't like your quitting something that you began."

For me this was truly the problem. You see, when I was a child, in my family, you just didn't quit. Anything! You didn't start a game of Monopoly unless you planned to finish it. You didn't quit just because the game went six hours. Quitting wasn't fair to the other players. No, you toughed it out. In the first eighteen years of my life (all the years I'd lived at home), the only thing I remember quitting was Cub Scouts. Even then I'd stuck it out for a whole year.

I somehow grew up believing that quitters were bad, unambitious people who never amounted to anything, vagrants not worth the cardboard they slept beneath.

Take Old Dicky, for example. Old Dicky our town drunk (who wasn't all that old), slouched against the town square World War II memorial stone, snoozing away hot summer afternoons. He'd been a quitter.

My grandpa said he remembered Dicky when he was younger. "Well, I'll tell you, Bobby, he wasn't the brightest kid I'd ever met, but he was a nice little boy till he started quittin'. Quit Little League. Quit Junior Firemen. Quit high school. Even quit work at the bottle plant. And for what? Just look at 'im now. If that's not the saddest excuse for a man I've ever seen. Just makes your heart ache."

And of course I knew you didn't have to look too far to find other examples. There was Al Capone and Oswald and that crazy guy who killed the nurses. They probably all quit junior high choir or confirmation or something.

Quitting revealed a basic flaw in one's character. Quitters didn't have the stuff to stick it out when the going got tough, and I told my son what my dad told me. "Nathan, if you're a quitter now, you'll be a quitter for the rest of your life, and you'll miss the rewards on the other side of the experience."

Even as I spoke, I was surprised how unconvincing I sounded to myself, and I was pretty sure I didn't fool my son either.

"Yeah, right, Dad."

He stared, and I waited. Strangely, I began to hope that this time he wouldn't back down.

I'd wanted to quit a bunch of things when I was his age, but I didn't. Now I think maybe I should have. I took math for four years in high school. Four years! Algebra, geometry, trigonometry, and calculus. I started to get lost about three weeks into my first freshman term and never really found my way out of the confusion. This continual floundering in the Pits of Pi caused tremendous stress and made me feel intellectually inept. I've never completely recovered.

In college I took Math 101 pass-fail, passed it by a hair (I don't know what that is in metrics), and have not opened a math book since.

Nowadays, of course, scientists and doctors recognize my condition. Now it's somewhat acceptable to say, "I'm sorry, but you'll have to help me. I can't figure out what my new insurance premium will come out to per month. You see I have M.D.S. (Math Deficiency Syndrome)." This is actually the absence of one algebraic gene or something. It's a right-brain, left-brain thing I don't entirely understand, probably because one of my sides is empty.

And Spanish! *¡Mi Gloria!* Why did I have to take four years of Spanish? Why couldn't I have taken two years like some of the other kids? No one spoke Spanish within three hundred miles of my town except maybe my Spanish teacher, and I don't think he spoke it very well. I know *I* couldn't understand a word he said.

Looking back I can't recognize any rewards for toughing it out. I should have quit. But it was too scary at the time. There were too many unanswered questions like, Would I end up sleeping over a heating vent or killing a cop? Would I have to marry someone in the eighth grade? Would people talk about Old Bobby sleeping against the World War II monument? Well, yes, probably. Those are the kinds of things that happen to quitters.

Now my son and I sat facing each other like two silent polygrams. (That's a geometric term for multi-sided objects, and this is a desperate attempt to apply the little I learned.)

I remember the first time I quit something on my own. I didn't do it very well.

I'd played high school football for four years, and surprisingly, I'd been fairly good. Surprising not because I lacked the talent or the size, but because I never really liked the game or the competition. But I enjoyed the team camaraderie and particularly the attention I received in my little town.

I was fortunate to play on teams that, by my senior year, had won twenty-three games in a row. So a number of my teammates and I received letters from interested college recruiters. The truth is I didn't have the desire or the talent to play even small college football. However, several colleges couldn't tell that from my game films, and I couldn't resist the flattering headlines on page two of our little town paper. I should have gotten out of the game when I had the opportunity to do so with honor, but I didn't even know how to quit when I had the chance.

So off I went to college in the middle of August, dreading the prospect of playing a game I didn't really like with guys who lived it with passion.

It turned out to be worse than I could have imagined. My first-year coach, Coach Vader (not his real name), was a maniac. You remember the great Woody Hayes when he went nuts on national TV and beat up one of his young players on the sidelines? Remember the great Bobby Knight, throwing a fit and tossing chairs out on to center court? Remember Jack Nicholson in every movie he's ever made? I think my coach studied that tape footage and learned from The Greats.

He was like that all the time. He berated us in practice. He screamed at us nonstop during meals, his face only inches from the side of our heads. We awakened in the dark each morning to his voice taunting us over the dormitory intercom. (Actually many of us had never gotten to sleep.)

It was so bad that two tri-captains, with distinguished college careers, quit on Friday, five days into the preseason. I only made it to Thursday.

I didn't even have the guts to talk to the coach. At 5:30 in the morning, on the way to the field house for ankle taping, I turned around, hopped a Chicago cab, and rode off into the sunrise.

The cabby said, "*¿A donde vas?*"

Of course I didn't understand, but it didn't matter. I wasn't in the mood for conversation.

"Take me to my aunt's in Brookfield," I said extra loud, presuming that the louder I spoke the better he might understand English.

We drove for an hour or so, and I began to wonder if José was not only driving me to my aunt's but also taking me for a ride. It seemed as though we passed the same shopping center quite a few times, though perhaps I'm wrong in thinking so. I suppose there could be a chain of Laundromats called Ronnie's One and Only Cleaner. Several hours later, we found my aunt's house. He collected a good portion of my fall tuition with a big smile and a "*¡Muchas gracias, senor!*"

I said the only Spanish that came to mind, "*Que sera, sera. Feliz Navidad.*"

I stayed with my aunt for a couple of weeks until school began. During that time I finally worked up the nerve to call my dad and tell him the news. I'd only been on my own for four days, and already I was a quitter.

He didn't understand. He gave me all the arguments against quitting. All the arguments, which, of course, I already knew. He even suggested I go back and talk to Coach Vader, tell him I'd made a mistake but I now realized how wrong I'd been and was willing to do anything to get back on the team. Tell him I just wanted to contribute any way I could.

Obviously my dad had not met my coach. I told him that what he suggested was impossible, and our conversation ended in silence.

I was a quitter, a failure.

In retrospect, I now think I did the right thing. My mistake was to begin in the first place. One plays college football for the love of the game, or at least for the love of the scholarship money, but I played for neither. I played because I didn't know how to stop. I didn't know that people would like me even if I wasn't a great athlete. But I found out the truth. By quitting football, I found something better.

I auditioned for and was chosen to sing in the college choir. I signed up to sing in a gospel folk group that represented my school. I played intramural football. I even *studied* and did well for the first time in my life, and I never had so much fun learning.

Now undoubtedly I would have discovered some of these things anyway. But quitting football made me take a hard look at myself and make some decisions about other things I wanted to do with my life.

Years later, here I sat with my son, who was staring at the wall, and I waited.

Then slowly, calmly, with resignation, looking me right in the eye, he said, "Dad, I blew it. I love basketball, but I don't like the competition at all. I know now that it's not something I want to pursue during my high school years. I liked the idea of wearing a uniform and getting a letter jacket and being an athlete, and I wish that I was, but it's never going to happen. It's just not me. I wish I'd known this before I began, but Dad, now I know that I just don't belong on the team."

I guess that is what I wanted to hear him say. "Okay, son. I think you should talk to your coach and tell him what you've told me."

I don't know. Maybe I did the wrong thing. Maybe in years to come I'll look back and realize that this was a time I should have held my ground and insisted he not be a quitter. But I don't think so.

First of all, it's getting a little harder for me to insist very often. The boy is fourteen years old, and it's become important for me to choose carefully those things I insist on and those things I let slide. Furthermore, his reasoning seemed sound to me.

The truth is he *was* playing ball for the wrong reasons. He had gone out for the team in an attempt to conform to the world, and what better way than to play basketball? In our society, athletes are highly regarded. Artists have a little tougher time finding their place. You can't "letter" in art of drama. You can't buy a little felt paintbrush, pottery wheel, or singing lips to sew on your varsity jacket. So some kids, like mine, try desperately to succeed in an area outside the natural gifts God has given them. Though he might not be able to put it into words, in quitting, Nate was choosing not to squeeze himself into the world's mold, and that is a good thing.

In allowing him to quit, I believe I was being responsible to "train him in the way he should go." I was allowing him to reject activities that take him away from his natural bent to choose others that are more in line with the many gifts God has given him.

As often happens in parenting, I wonder if Nate and I did the right thing. At the moment, though, I feel good about our decision.

Later that day four inches of snow fell on Lower Mundane.

"Finish your dessert, boys, and then I could use your help shoveling off the driveway."

True to his nature, our youngest son, Lars, was enthusiastic. And true to *his*, Nathan began to bargain.

"I'll tell you what, Dad," he said with a sly smile. "We'll help you with the drive if, when we're done, you'll shoot some hoops with us."

I told him he had a deal.

CHAPTER EIGHTEEN

Confessions of a Fliphead

Several weeks ago Nate and I stopped by the Old Corner Store for a gallon of milk. At the cash register we stood behind Srini Ramanujan, a small, elderly woman whom I believe is of East Indian descent. I'm not certain how she came to live here, and it's not likely she will ever share her story with me as she speaks very little English and seems to understand even less.

She stood in front of us with a large shopping cart, the only one in town. It belongs to her. Every Tuesday she rolls it from her little home about a block away and then rolls it back again with another week's supplies. Today I could see nearly one-third of the cart was filled with a colorful harvest of tiny spice bottles. This surprised me not at all.

I learned where she lives while delivering for Meals on Wheels. Even as I knocked on Srini's door, I suspected I was in trouble as a warm pocket of spicy air enveloped my head. My nose began to run. My eyes started to water.

Frantically waving the fumes away, I tried to retreat, but it was too late. The door opened, and through my tears, I saw the blurry figure of little Mrs. Ramanujan standing with her instrument of torture, a sizzling pan of something burnt.

One needs to understand that I am Scandinavian and thus posses a culinary heritage that celebrates the bland and colorless. I think the strongest spice in my genetic vocabulary is some kind of fish.

As smoke from Srini's meal blew into my face, the experience was reminiscent of the time in junior high when Tommy Landow sprayed a can of Mace in the shower room.

Now standing behind her in the checkout line, I calculated she had filled her cart with enough granular energy to heat most of Lower Mundane in the middle of March. I held in *my* hand one (just one!) plastic gallon jug of milk. I tried to ask her if I might go ahead.

"Mrs. Ramanujan," I said, cheerily holding my gallon of milk in front of me, "do you mind if I go ahead of you?"

She didn't understand.

"I have just this one jug," I reasoned more loudly. "You have so-o-o-o many things." I gestured with a sweeping arm movement over her cart. Then, for contrast, shrugging my shoulders and holding my index finger close to my smiling face, I begged in a little voice, "I have just one!"

Her eyes lit up. "Oh ho, I see! I see. No, no, I no need milk. Okey-dokey! Okey-dokey!"

If Donny Barnes had been working the register, I would have said, "Hey, Donny, help me out here," and he probably would have. But this day, a tough-looking young woman I didn't know inspected each tiny bottle for a price tag and punched in the numbers. Behind me Nate laughed aloud as he leafed through a copy of a tabloid that appeared to be a cousin of the *National Enquirer*.

"Hey, Dad." He snorted, holding the front page toward me. "Check this out."

Beneath a headline appeared a picture of Phil Donahue with his arm around something that looked like a geriatric, white-haired ET.

"Can you even imagine anyone believing this stuff?" I said, scanning the article. "I mean, who would buy one of these? Even if Phil Donahue *was* sired by an alien, I'm not going to pay a buck to read about it. And besides," I said, pointing at a paragraph, "it says right here that Phil refused comment."

"Yeah, Dad," Nate teased, "but they always refuse comment. If that's not an admission of guilt, I don't know what is. And look on the next page. Did you know that JFK was really a woman?"

"Well now, son," I mocked, "you can't believe everything you read. Personally I choose not to believe that particular story. And besides, even if he was, she was still a fine president."

The lady at the register eyed us with a reprimanding stare, which clearly meant, "If you read it, you buy it!" She punched in a price for the last bottle of curry powder and pointed out the total to Mrs. Ramanujan, who fumbled through her purse for the correct change.

"Oh, Dad," Nate blurted out, "look at this one!"

On an inside page was a picture of an Asian couple in full hospital garb holding a newborn. Above, the headline

read "Baby Born with Electrical switch on Side of Head."
Beneath, we read the following:

> *Shanghai*
> *Chinese governmental officials confirmed reports*
> *Friday that baby Ping, daughter of Mr. And Mrs. Wong*
> *Pong, was born last week with an electrical circuit breaker*
> *attached to the side of her head. Commenting on the*
> *strange occurrence, attending physician Dr. Ho Wee Kow*
> *said, "We unscrewed the plastic face plate and found that*
> *the fixture itself was manufactured by Eelectrozap of*
> *Sterling, Kans. I was quite surprised. This is the first such*
> *occurrence in my career."*
>
> *Officials believe the switch is connected to the baby's*
> *brain. In the "on" position, Baby Ping is a normal, happy*
> *infant. However, when the circuit breaker is flipped off, she*
> *enters a comatose state.*
>
> *The baby's mother, speaking through translators, said,*
> *"We feel blessed to have such a special child. We feel she*
> *is normal in every way. And thanks to the switch, she's*
> *already sleeping well through the night."*

I could hear Nate chortling as he leaned against my
shoulder, reading along. Despite the story's obvious
absurdity, it touched something within me that left me
feeling dazed. Inexplicably, something in it seemed
plausible.

"That'll be a dollar twenty-five." It was the cashier.
"You want the paper too?"

A strange, unsolicited thought brushed my
consciousness. The Chinese baby, little Ping Pong, is not

alone. This is not an isolated case. Oh, yes, perhaps she is the first child to have the switch attached to the outside of the head, but how many like myself have long ago discovered a switch just beneath the skin?

"I said, that'll be a dollar twenty-five. Do you want the paper you've already read?"

I stood staring at the tabloid. The lady stood staring at me.

"Dad," Nate said, poking me in the side, "come on, let's go."

"Uh, yeah, sure." I said, tossing the paper on the counter, "I'll take it."

At home we laughed again, perhaps even harder, as we read the tabloid for Judy and Lars. I laughed this time too as we read about the baby, but the article had revealed more to me than its author could have intended.

Please understand that I don't believe the story is true. I think it was probably conceived by the same guy who wrote "Dolphin Grows Human Arms—Learns American Sign Language." But the story sparked within me the memory of discovering my own circuit breaker, and the truth of my own story is indisputable.

I've written previously of the little church from my boyhood. I've told about Helmer Larson' peppermints, and I've stated he was one of the main reasons I mostly looked forward to going to church. I used the word "mostly," for a part of me resisted our Sunday morning ritual.

"Morning glory! Rise and shine!" my mother sang cheerily, peeking into my bedroom.

I ignored her.

"Hey, young man, breakfast is ready, and Sunday school starts in twenty-five minutes. So up you go right now!"

I got up, eyes closed, and shuffled toward the bathroom, dragging one twisted foot of my new jammies a few inches behind my heel. There was no reason to protest. I'd tried that before, and it wouldn't work.

On Sunday mornings I went to Sunday school and church with my family and that was that; unless of course I was sick. Sickness was defined as strep throat, measles, mumps, diarrhea, vomiting, or a temperature. At four years of age, I was unable to simulate any of these maladies.

Any symptoms leading up to these sicknesses were unacceptable excuses. So, for example you couldn't just feel poorly (nausea), you had to actually throw up (nausea climaxis). You couldn't just have a scratchy throat. Uh-uh. The doctor had to stick it with a Popsicle stick and say, "Ah-hah, lots of this stuff going around."

Now, removing my toothbrush from its Howdy Doody holder and squeezing a gnarl of paste, I was resigned. It was Sunday morning, and I was going to have to go to church with my family again.

Sunday school was not a problem, because it seemed to be just for my friends and me, with colorful Bible comics, coloring books, flannel-graphed stories, and even snacks. I'd probably get out of bed all by myself to go to Sunday school.

No, Sunday school was not the problem. The problem was church.

The first half of the service was bearable, because we did plenty of ups and downs. Up for a hymn, down for a prayer, up for a response, down for a hymn, up for a prayer, down for an offering. Maybe even up for a trip to the bathroom. But then the pastor said something like, "This morning we open to the fifteenth chapter of..." and things got really rough.

First, I don't think my pastor lost any sleep on Saturday night praying that his sermon might communicate effectively to my preschool buddies or me. Furthermore, the pew did not fit my body. It wasn't that I didn't know how to sit properly like a big boy. I'd been working on that for a couple of years. But any skills I'd developed in this area were lost when applied to our church pews.

The benches were apparently not designed to be sat upon. They were uncushioned, straight backed, straight seated, and polished weekly to a high gloss. If I sat with my back flat against the back of the pew, as my parents' raised eyebrows encouraged me to do, then the hard edge of the seat caught me right above my ankles and made my feet go numb.

This became a mysterious occurrence for me. I had been struggling to make sense of much that I was hearing during worship. I'd gleaned a fair amount concerning the Holy Spirit. Of course, there was much I didn't understand, but one thing I knew for sure, God's Holy Spirit desired to come into my heart, my soul.

I was pretty sure that's what he was trying to do every Sunday morning as I felt the prickly sensation entering my toes. This was the only place and the only time I felt the sensation. It had to be the Spirit. And what better way to enter my sole, I reasoned, than right down through my toes.

When the prickling became too much to bear, I'd squirm a little lower. This caused my bottom to slip off the seat and my head to clunk the back of the pew before I found myself noisily deposited on the hardwood floor, looking at rows of pressed pant legs and old lady shoes.

Then my parents would lift me back on the pew. Again my feet would turn blue, and the process would continue for about thirty-five minutes, nearly an eternity for a four-year-old.

Finally I would hear the pastor say, "Let's pray," or "Amen," after which I would gratefully stand with my parents for the final hymn and benediction.

I had no complaints about Sunday school. Church was the problem.

Now, having pulled on my clothes and snapped on my bowtie all by myself, I stared into a bowl of Cheerios and wished I could get very sick for just a couple of hours.

If I could just get a few mumps, I thought, and with my elbo on the table, I rested my head on my fist.

Wham! I flew into an imaginary world. Everything was cool and moist. I was floating, and the doctor was there too.

"Uh-huh... could be," he said to my mother while thumping two fingers on my back. "Looks, ma'am, like your son has a good case of the strepped mumps. I count about half a dozen on his back and one behind his ear. Very contagious, and they could be catchy too. You can expect he'll probably throw up, little diarrhea, maybe a measly rash, but it should clear up by noon. And then the best thing would be to let him play outdoors for the rest of the day. Yep, lots of exercise and fun, that's the best thing. In the meantime, you and your husband probably ought to get to church. The boy'll be fine. I've got him floating inside that cheerio right there. That's the best thing for him now… just let him cool down in a nice bowl of milk."

Then I heard my dad's voice.

"Hey, buddy, let's get that shoe tied. Wipe your chin there, and we're off like a dirty shirt."

"What?" I said, shaking the vivid image away.

"I said, let's get this shoe tied or we're going to be late."

Incredible! I'd been sitting looking into my cereal and then almost magically I was floating inside a cheerio, cool milk lapping my armpits, soothing the mumps on my back. What had happened? What fun!

Two hours later, sitting in the pew, I heard the pastor say, "Today we open to the…" I rested my elbow on my knee, leaned my head on my fist, and wham! I entered a new dimension deep within my imagination. I knew it wasn't a dream because I wasn't sleeping, and besides it was just like real. I swam through liquid blue. I flew high above Old Baldy, the wind blowing down the back of my shirt. I discovered big dinosaur bones in my backyard, and magic sparkling spider webs beneath the front porch. I could hear the sermon, but it didn't come through very strongly. The minister sounded like a small tinny voice transmitted through my little transistor radio.

Twenty-five minutes later when the pastor said, "Let us pray," every head bowed but mine. Mine shot right up. The service was over! Minutes later I was past the pastor and outside with my friends. It was like a miracle.

From that moment on I became dependent on the switch. My teachers wrote on my report card that I had a tendency to daydream from time to time. They didn't realize the severity of my condition. None of them suspected that I was a Fliphead.

I learned quickly to control myself during school. If I flipped the switch in class, I'd pay at test time. But in church there weren't any tests, so there didn't seem to be any consequences. The sermons became painless. I had a good time, and my parents were pleased that I sat so still like a big boy.

Of course that was the problem. I was sitting like a big boy. And when I became a big boy, that's still the way I sat. Oh, by that time, of course, I was far more sophisticated with the switch. I didn't need to even rest my head anymore. I didn't have to stare off into space anymore. No one even knew I'd flipped the switch.

In fact, I hadn't flipped it. It had flipped all by itself, automatically triggered by a sequence of words. "We turn today to chapter..." or "Our Scripture text this morning is..." or "the words of the apostle Paul speaking to the..." All I had to do was hear these phrases, and I was gone.

Then I'd hear, "Shall we pray," or "In closing let's turn to hymn number..." or of course, "Amen," and the switch would flip back.

I could smile and chuckle at the pastor's jokes. I could look concerned, prayerful, or contemplative. I could shake the pastor's hand at the door and say, "Wonderful sermon!" But I'd never heard a thing, and no one even knew.

In college I had a professor with a lateral lisp that made all of his S's sound like soft X's. "Welcome to Sxoxial Sxiencxe 101. Pleasxe take your sxeatsx."

I nearly missed my midterm when he announced, "Our tesxt today will be graded on a curve." I only heard the first three words, "Our tesxt today," and the switch flipped as it had so many times before I'd have missed the whole exam had he not finished the sentence with, "will be graded on a curve." A struggling fellow student saved my neck by shouting, "Amen!"

It's a day-to-day struggle for me now. I've pretty much had to face this thing on my own, deprogramming, preparing for certain word sequences, holding my finger firmly pushed against my temple to keep the switch from flipping automatically. (Ironically, this makes me look more intelligent and aware than I really am.)

Most importantly I pray a lot. I ask God to help me focus. I ask him to reveal himself to me through the preaching of the word. I'm happy to say that he very often does.

Well, that's my confession. If there is anyone else out there who understands what I'm talking about, I hope my sharing has been an encouragement to you. I want you to know that you're not alone.

If I hadn't read that stupid article, I might never have faced up to my problem. I might never have been able to look someone in the eye and say, ""Hello, my name is Bob, and I'm a Fliphead."

CHAPTER NINETEEN

Ice on the Old Oak:

A Seasonal Dilemma

There is a time for everything,
and a season for every activity under heaven.

(Ecclesiastes 3:1)

We slept very little last night. It's not that we weren't tired, it's just that sleep is hard to find when outside your window the planet sounds as if it is falling apart. This interesting phenomenon occurs at least once a winter here in our little river community.

I believe the same geographical complexion that brings us stifling humidity all summer gives us dense fog during much of the winter. When this cold grayness continues for days or even weeks, it can permeate one's spirit with a chilling oppression. However, if the temperature drops rapidly, it can have quite the opposite effect.

When the fog freezes, it transforms our town into a sparkling, crystalline sculpture. It's most beautiful if it happens before the first snowfall, when each blade of grass is glazed upright with a thin laminate of delicate ice. Dried roses and autumn mums display their muted colors beneath a frozen veneer glistening with white morning sunlight. The net on the basketball hoop hangs resplendent, gilded like a Faberge masterpiece. Even the old gutted '65 Rambler behind my neighbor's garage takes on a glory not beheld since its showroom days.

Don't bother going down to the Old Corner Store for film. On these mornings, it's sold out by ten. For at least a few hours, and sometimes as long as a week, Lower Mundane is a photographer's paradise.

I love these days mostly for their visual beauty but also for the fragile sounds that surround our home. With the slightest whisper of breeze, ice glitters down through our trees with tiny, glass-tubed percussion melodies.

Of course, as is always the case, there is a fee for such beauty. Though the sand trucks are out early on these special mornings, still there are numerous fender benders. And usually an old person breaks a hip on the perilous walk from the kitchen door to the garage. Even so, most of them blame themselves and insist these exquisite icy days are still what they've always loved most about winters here.

But there can be too much of a good thing. Sometimes when the fog is particularly heavy and there is no breeze, more than an inch of ice forms on every branch, limb, and twig. Then late at night a strong wind blows in from the northwest, and the beauty comes crashing down, bringing much of the tree with it. This is why we had such trouble sleeping last evening.

We built our new home beneath a grand white oak, which has inhabited our lot for at least a century. Unquestionably the most impressive tree in the area, it is the primary reason we bought the property. Surely it had weathered heavy ice storms scores of times, but there is a limit to what even so great a creation as this can endure.

All night long it moaned and showered our home with ice pellets. One by one it snapped its bending upper branches in a sacrificial attempt to shed the heavy burden. And it was not alone in its struggle. In the darkness of our room, we stared toward the ceiling and listened to the eerie, shrieking destruction of trees all over town.

After the storm, in the stillness of early morning, we sadly surveyed the damage. From our bedroom window, we could see clear down the hillside and up the river valley. Most of the hardwoods—the oaks, cherries, and maples— had lost their upper third. Most of the soft woods—the box elders and poplars—lay nearly horizontal. All the evergreens drooped like sad frowns. Thankfully, compared to the rest anyway, our old oak fared well.

The lawn was strewn with small branches. Beside the house lay piles of ice nuggets like discarded cartridges from the long night's siege, but the tree looked pretty good. No main branches had come down nor had the trunk split like many others. In fact, I could spot only one major problem. A huge limb, nearly a third of the tree, rested frozen to our kitchen roof.

We were surprised to find our electricity working, so while Judy put on some coffee, I slid stiff-legged across our deck to survey for potential damage. From beneath, the situation concerned me even more. It appeared as if the end of the massive limb and all its smaller bushy branches were permanently welded to the shingles and gutter. I didn't like its being there. Undoubtedly it had sagged like this often during the last century, but never before had my home been in the way.

I went back inside to find Judy in the kitchen. Pouring a hot cup of coffee, I said to her, "Well, I don't like that branch lying up there."

"Why?" she asked. "It doesn't seem to be doing any harm."

"Not now," I agreed. "But if the wind kicks up again, I can just picture that limb coming down and bringing a big pile of shingles with it. Then we'd really have a problem when all this ice starts to melt."

"Well, whether it does or not," she said, clearly hoping to discourage my endeavor, "there's not much you can do about it. You could break your neck if you tried to go up there. I think you should be patient. Just relax and let it melt."

That was not what I wanted to hear. You see, I am not a particularly patient person. When there is a problem, I like to deal with it right away. I like to fix it quickly so it won't get worse. I don't like to wonder what the outcome will be. I want order and wholeness in my life, and it bothers me when things around me are chaotic and splintered. If I don't fix things as they happen, I feel like the old oak, breaking apart, frantically trying to shed a burden that has become too great.

Some problems can be solved or even avoided if they're dealt with promptly. This is not to suggest that it's easy, just better. If the roof is leaking into the attic, it may not be easy to fix now, but it will certainly be much harder to repair later. Then you'll have to fix it and the living room ceiling.

When I hear that someone has said something dishonest about me, it's not easy to call that person, but it's much better to deal with it directly before the gossip erodes other relationships too.

When I've unintentionally wronged someone, I can't sit through a meal before I've called to apologize. It's just the way I am.

The dilemma, for me, occurs when I confront the kind of problems that can't be solved quickly. I still want them fixed now.

"You know," I said to my wife, "we spent a bundle of bucks on that roof and this wood ceiling and these kitchen windows. I don't want to take a chance on that wind whipping up again."

"Bob," she asserted sternly, placing her hands on her hips just like my mom used to do, "this could end up like the time you tried to fix the bathroom sink."

"Aw, come on, Jude!" I protested. "You got a brand new sink, didn't you?"

"Yes," she confessed, "but we didn't want a new sink. Remember? We couldn't afford a new sink. Remember? But you smashed the old one so we had no choice. And what about the time you tried to fix the television?"

"Aw, come on, Judy! You got a brand new TV, didn't you?"

"Yes, yes! Exactly!" she said, gesturing wildly. "I did, and I've gotten a lot of new things I wasn't expecting and didn't budget for. Do you see a pattern here?"

We were clearly having a problem, and I would have loved to fix it, but I do things in an orderly manner. The tree problem came first so that would have to be dealt with first. When I finished on the roof we would handle this little misunderstanding.

"Honey, I promise I'll be careful," I said and headed for the garage.

Everything was covered with thick ice. The garage was sealed shut, and the whining automatic door-opener needed my help to haul its extra-heavy load. Half an hour later, having determined that the smoking door-opener might have to be replaced, I grabbed the roof ladder and carefully made my way across the back lawn. Beneath the kitchen window but safely to the side of the limb, I shattered two deep holes in the grass to hold the ladder's feet. Then I climbed carefully ten feet to the gutter and appraised the situation.

I was pleased to see that far less branch rested on the roof than I had earlier supposed. In fact, only about six inches clung to the edge. The rest was mostly thick, dried leaves, giving the impression of more substance than they actually had. I needed only to break the icy weld and slide the last few inches free. If it did sag a bit lower, the leaves and twigs would do no damage to the house even if they scraped against the kitchen window.

I bumped the limb carefully with the butt of my hand. It didn't move. I tried a little harder. This time, slowly, the frozen bond began to give way. One more nudge, and it would be free.

Surprisingly I didn't need to touch it again. As if awakening from a cold hibernation, the branch shuddered slightly and began to move slowly, almost imperceptibly, toward the gutter.

At this moment, odd images from my past began to flood my mind. Seemingly disparate objects appeared before my eyes —a sink, a television, a new engine for my Volkswagen Rabbit, my children's bowl of goldfish, an overheated garage door-opener. The tree slid sluggishly lower.

The overly burdened branch dropped off the edge and, still slowly without any acceleration, ripped the gutter and the bottom row of shingles off the roof. Down the roofline, the gutter supports popped one nail at a time, like a spoiled child ripping the buttons off a Sunday shirt. As I stared in disbelief, the branch continued to sag.

Back at the base of the tree I heard a deep, painful moan. Then a long, searing crack tore loudly, twelve feet down the trunk. The shiny white wood lay exposed like a compound fracture. Finally the branch rested on the ground.

I was sickened by what I saw, and it had nothing to do with the gutter. That could be replaced. But the tree... that was a different story. It had weathered storms for more than a century, and I had destroyed it in seconds. I felt weakened with a sudden grief like I did as a small boy watching my dog dart into the road and under the wheels of the passing milk truck. I felt shaken like I did as a young adolescent watching my cousin fall from the high branches of a tree and disappear through the piney boughs beneath me. My dog died the next day. Thankfully my cousin survived. Perhaps the tree would too, though it would show this scar forever and never again display its former symmetry. A third of it was gone now, and it was my fault.

I left the gutter where it hung and walked inside. Judy had seen it all. She sat silently in the living room with her face turned away. She looked out the window, and she wept. Surely she was angry, frustrated, and aching with "I told you so's." All of it would be expressed soon enough. Now though, she grieved as I did for what I had destroyed.

Even as I stared out the window I could see the ice melting. If I had left the branch alone, most likely it would have been fine. But I'm not a patient person. If ever I doubt that to be true, I need only look out the kitchen window. The proof is before my eyes. Unfortunately it is also before the eyes of anyone else who cares to look, and it is their loss as well.

The only redemption in this story is that God is present here too and eager to teach me, however painfully obvious the lesson may be. I stare at what was once a magnificent tree, and I hear the voice of its Creator saying,

"There is a time to react and a time to heed counsel.
There is a time to fix and a time to let be.
There is a time to take things into your own hands,
And a time to leave things in mine."

I am slowly learning the art of discerning one season from the other.

A *Letter for Rosie*

Rosie Serillo stood at the door of her apartment, looking just a little confused. Next to her, smiling broadly for the camera and extending a letter in her direction, stood our postmaster Pierce Butler. The photograph appeared on the front page of the Lower Mundane *Reporter Argus*. Above the picture a headline read "Better Late Than Never." Beneath appeared the following story.

Ninety-six-year-old Rosie Serillo of River Bend Manor, received a letter Friday morning. This would not be newsworthy had the letter not been sent in 1923. When Postmaster Pierce Butler apologized for the seventy-year delay, Rosie commented, "Well, I know you fellows get busy down there."

The letter, affixed with a one-cent stamp, was mailed June 6, 1923, but never made it out of the sorting room. On June 4, 1993, a carpenter found it behind a piece of floor molding removed during post office renovations. Postmaster Butler said it could have been delivered Wednesday, June 5, but he decided to wait one more day to make it exactly seventy years.

The letter had no return address but still bore a red wax seal in the shape of a tulip. It was mailed to Ms. Serillo at her present residence, River Bend Manor, Lower Mundane. The River Bend Manor it referred to, though, was the estate built by Rosie's father, Carmen Serillo, in 1904, later owned by Ms. Serillo's brother-in-law, the late Ross Rossi, and destroyed by fire in 1930. The new river Bend Manor, a home for senior citizens, was built on the same location with funds provided by Rosie's sister, Winifred Rossi. Ms. Serillo moved back to River Bend Manor, as its first new resident, last year.

Late Friday afternoon, when asked by phone about the contents of the letter, Ms. Serillo commented only that it was of a personal nature.

The same summer the letter was sent, Ms. Serillo was engaged to be married to Albert Farmelo. Farmelo died July 8 during the flu epidemic of 1923, which claimed the lives of fifteen residents in our community.

Rosie Serillo remained unmarried and has lived in Lower Mundane all of her ninety-six years.

Of course people speculated on the contents of the envelope, wondering with fascination what it would be like to read a love letter from your betrothed seventy years after that person's death. But Rosie offered no more information, and no one pushed her further.

About a week later I was awakened early to the smell of cardamom bread rising sweetly in our kitchen. I knew immediately Judy had risen earlier still, and someone in our town was in for a treat. Minutes later, I cut into a fresh loaf and melted a knife full of soft butter onto a slice.

"Well," I said, folding the tasty morsel into my mouth, "who's the lucky recipient of your early morning labor?"

"Do you mean besides you?" she teased.

I poured a cup of coffee and buttered another piece. With a fat, quilted, mitten, Judy opened the oven door and carefully lifted out a rack bearing two more loaves of yeasty fragrance.

"I woke up early thinking about Rosie," she said. "Could you cut me a couple of white roses off the bush to take along? And make sure you get a few new buds so she can enjoy them for a while."

"I'd be happy to ride along with you," I offered. "I've got to stop by the hardware store this morning anyway."

"Oh, that would be great," she said excitedly. "Rosie never complains when I visit by myself, but I know it's special for her when you come along."

Half an hour later we pulled into the lovely, landscaped circular drive at River Bend Manor. As we stepped out of the car, the automatic sprinklers popped their heads from beneath the sod and began to cool the flowerbeds, already wilting in the hot morning sun.

On the way through the lobby, I glanced briefly into the newly finished Rossi Reading room. On the wall hung a commissioned oil-painted portrait of the young Ross and Winifred Rossi. Ross sat confidently, his thick black hair slicked back, a pencil mustache highlighting his handsome smile. He looked remarkably like Clark Gable or perhaps early photos of a young Howard Hughes. His left hand gently braced the elbow of his much younger wife, who looked every bit as wealthy and beguiling as the movie starlets of her day. She smiled too.

Oddly, this took us both by surprise. Though we had only lived in this community for a couple of years, we had seen Winifred often but never had we seen her smile.

Judy commented, "You know, even so she looks unhappy."

We walked past the nurses' station to Rosie's door where Judy tapped, "Ta, ta, tata... ta... ta." There was no response. "Ta, ta, tata, ta."

I opened the door part way and called softly, "Rosie?"

Entering through the short, unlit hallway, we could see Rosie sitting in her living room chair.

Leaning forward, Judy announced again, "Hello, Rosie."

Rosie looked up in surprise. "Oh my goodness!" she replied sweetly, preparing to lift herself out of the chair. "Well, come in. I wasn't expecting you. Come in."

"You don't have to get up," Judy said, putting an arm around Rosie's shoulder and easing her back down. "We can only stay a minute. We just wanted to bring you some flowers and a little treat." She handed me the bread and went to the kitchen for a vase.

"I'll tell you, Rosie, that woman of mine's been up baking since the crack of dawn. She wanted me to mail this loaf from the post office, but I told her I wouldn't do it. 'No way!' I said, 'Judy, you know how it is with Rosie and the post office. If we drive it out to River Bend Manor, she can probably have some for lunch. But if we *mail* it, even if we send it first class, we're talking clear into the next century before she'll get a taste.'"

Rosie laughed quietly, girlishly covering her mouth with one hand and waving me away with the other.

Judy placed the vase of roses on the television, where they were drenched in the morning sunlight that poured through the patio door. "So, my friend," Judy said, sitting on the old ottoman at Rosie's feet, "how have you been?"

"Winnie was here," Rosie replied flatly, almost in a whisper.

For a moment no one spoke. I looked at Judy quizzically. Could she mean her sister, Winifred? Winifred, who had not spoken to her for six decades? Winifred, who bore a nearly demented, inexplicable hatred toward her older sister?

"I'm sorry, Rosie," Judy said, "but did you say Winnie?"

"My sister," Rosie confirmed, and her eyes filled with tears.

Judy snapped a tissue out of a box on the coffee table and tenderly tucked it in Rosie's hand.

"She came by last week." Rosie said, removing her glasses and wiping her eyes. "My nephew Russel came with her. They didn't even knock. Just walked right in. First words out of her mouth were, 'Where is the letter?'"

"What letter, Rosie?" Judy asked.

"The old one," she said, motioning toward the coffee table. "The one they made such a fuss about in the paper."

"Rosie," I asked, "why would she want your letter?"

"That's what I asked her, but she wouldn't answer. She looked everywhere, under the bed, in all my drawers and cupboards. I told her the letter was none of her business. When she couldn't find it, she just walked out. We… we…" Grief caught in Rosie's throat. "We hadn't seen each other face to face for so many years, and she wouldn't even call me by name."

I watched as anger filled Judy's eyes. "That makes me so mad. What makes her think she has the right to come barging into someone else's home?"

Rosie replaced her glasses and composed herself. Lifting her Bible from the coffee table, she said, "I finally know why my sister has hated me all these years."

She opened the front cover and retrieved an old envelope. "Go ahead," she said, handing us the letter. "You can read it."

We sat together, gazing at the artifact.

"Go ahead," she encouraged. "The letter is not from Albert. It's from Winnie."

The yellowed envelope had hardened with age much like she who had sent it. Turning it over I could see the remains of the red wax seal, cracked and soiled from seven decades of delay. I removed the letter as Judy sat beside me on the sofa. Together we read the lovely scrolled handwriting of a much lovelier Winifred. A Winifred who had not yet surrendered to the bitterness that would characterize her life.

On a June day in 1923, she sat in the opulence of her hillside home and wrote:

My Dear Sister Rosie,
I have begun this letter often but never have I been able to finish it. Today I will try again, and

this time I must succeed. Perhaps it will cause confusion and pain. If so, I am sorry, but confusion and pain have been frequent visitors here.

First let me say that I love you all very much. You are still my family, and I am so sorry for all that has come between us. I have made some poor decisions in my life. I wish to do so no longer. I fear that father's prediction has come to pass. My marriage has indeed caused all of us much pain. In spite of this, believe me, I still love my husband. Sometimes I wish I did not. Dare I say there are times I feel I should suffer the shame and leave him to return home. But I fear for my children and all that would mean.

You may not know that Ross has long forbidden me to speak to any of you. Why this is so I cannot say with certainty, but, Sister, please understand me when I say that he can be very persuasive. I dare not say more. Surely he would never condone my writing to you now, and I am doing so without his knowledge and in fear.

Believe me, I do not approve of my husband's endeavor to buy River Bend Manor. I know he has stated that, should the purchase transpire, Father may remain there for the rest of his life. I suspect that would not happen.

Furthermore, I am greatly concerned that my husband's wealth is derived from illegal, even sinister sources. Often I fear for his life. Often I fear for us all.

Throughout all of this, my greatest distress

(should I say torment?) is that my husband may be deliberately misleading me and separating me from you whom I love the most.

This brings me to my reason for writing, even at some risk. Rosie, Ross has told me of your dalliance. He has described to me in painful detail my own beloved sister's relentless pursuit of his affections. He has also confessed his failure to withstand the temptations of your beauty. He has asked me to forgive him, and I want to do so.

You have always been more beautiful than I. That is no secret. I cannot blame him. I know he is only a man. He has also told me of your visits here in my own home, even while I recovered from the birth of Ross, Jr. My heart does not want to believe what my mind says is true.

Please, Rosie, I write these words through a river of tears. I don't want to believe it. I know how deeply and how long you have loved Albert. I beg of you, tell me it is still so. Because at times I have come to doubt my husband's honesty, I have hope in my heart that this too is just part of his plan to estrange me from all of you.

Still I confess that imagining you with my husband has caused me to feel such hatred toward the older sister I have always cherished. My heart is breaking. I beg of you, Rosie, you must tell me the truth. I must hear it from your own lips. If I learn it is so, I surely will suffer no more than I am now. If I learn it is a lie, I will know for certain my husband's deceit. Then I don't know what I shall do.

I still love my husband, Rosie. I love my little children.

Ross will be leaving for business Sunday evening. There will be no one here on Monday morning but the children and me. It will be safe for you to come. Please meet me here at eight, and we shall talk.

If you don't arrive, I will accept that as your confession. I pray that will not happen. I don't believe it will. Please come!

Lovingly, Your Sister,
Winnie

Judy held the letter in her hand as we stared at the last line together. Snapping a tissue for herself, Judy said, "You never got the letter."

Confirming the obvious, Rosie nodded sadly.

"And if you had" I asked awkwardly. "I'm sorry, Rosie, but what if you *had* received the letter?"

"If I had," she answered, waving off my embarrassment, "I would have been on her doorstep early that Monday morning. I would have brought her flowers.

"Ross Rossi was an even worse man than we suspected. I'm so thankful that my father never knew Winnie was mistreated. It would have haunted him until his dying day. Ross Rossi was a very bad man. It wasn't enough for him to steal our wealth. He had to destroy our family too."

"So all these years," Judy said, moving back to the ottoman and grasping Rosie's silky hand, "Winifred has imagined you with her husband."

Rosie clutched Judy's hand in both of hers, and a soft distant smile crossed her face. "Yes, and of course it's not true. I was so smitten with my young sweetheart. I loved Albert more than anyone could have known. I would never have looked at another man. I never even *thought* of another man."

She paused for a moment, and a sweet sadness crossed her eyes. Speaking very slowly she said, "I have never *since* thought of another man."

"Rosie," I asked, "how did Winifred know it was her letter?"

"I'm sure she knew the moment she read the article. When we were little girls..." Rosie paused, reaching into the coffee table drawer, "Father gave both of us a letter seal."

She placed the stamp in my hand. "Mine was a rose," she said, turning it over so I could see the tiny flower. "Winnie's was a tulip. That's how Winnie knew it was her letter."

"But, Rosie," Judy said, "why would she want it now, after all these years?"

It was the words, "after all these years," that triggered what we could not have foreseen. Even Rosie seemed surprised, her countenance darkening as if a cloud had passed by the patio door. Like a selfish child she snatched the letter from Judy's hand. "Please," she said, on a precipice of sudden tears, "I'm sorry, but that's mine!"

"Oh yes, Rosie," Judy assured her gently, "of course it's yours."

For a moment Rosie struggled, rocking from side to side, unable to speak, her breath stolen by unexpected grief.

When she did speak it was little more than a harsh whisper. "Why would she want it now? Because I'm the only one who knows the truth about her husband." She clutched the pages like a weapon. "Now I have it in writing! He was a *bad* man! And Winnie is a *very... very...*" She began to sob. "... bad woman!"

Anger bent her features as seventy years of pain implored revenge, but courageously she would not give in. while Judy knelt beside her, Rosie fought the spirits that had enslaved her for so long. Dark stormy memories from decades of loneliness and depression roared about her. Wave after nauseous wave washed over her, but Rosie would not surrender. Finally, after what seemed a long while, they slowly retreated, and it was done.

Holding her gently, Judy comforted, "It's okay, it's okay."

Several minutes later Rosie reached up and patted Judy's cheek. She took a deep cleansing breath and smiled sadly.

"For fifty years," she said, "Winnie has been building monuments to her husband. The Rossi Reading room, Rossi Community Center, Rossi Memorial Library. Perhaps she thought if she named enough things after him, even so many years after his death, he might still somehow become a good man. I feel so bad for her. It's hard to believe she controlled most all of my life. And now... now can you imagine? Because I have this little letter, my sister is afraid of *me!*"

"Rosie," I asked cautiously, "what will you do with it?"

"Well," she said without hesitation, "I'm sorry I didn't give it back to her when she came. It doesn't belong here. It gives me bad feelings, and there is no longer room for them in my heart."

She scooched toward the edge of her chair and, reaching into the coffee table drawer, removed some stationery and a pen. Then she began to write, stopping every couple of words to speak. "Sometimes I am so disappointed in myself," she complained. "I should have told Winnie I loved her when she was here. Why I should have had some tulips picked for her when she came. That's what I should have done. But old stubborn me!"

As she spoke, her aged hand carefully formed the letters and spelled the words she would have spoken so long ago. "Poor, poor Winnie," she said. "She's hated me for so long. Now she fears that she may have been wrong. What a terrible burden!"

At the bottom of the page she scrawled her name. "There!" she said. "You asked me what I was going to do?" She handed me the note. "Well there it is."

I read her words, written in large brittle curves.

My Dear Sister Winnie,

Here is your letter. I'm so sorry. I have only ever loved Albert. This is the truth.

Please come again, for everything is forgiven.

Everything is forgiven.
Lovingly, Your Sister,
Rosie

I handed the note to Judy and gazed with wonder on our beautiful old friend. This face, which only moments before had grappled such darkness, now shone with more radiance than the morning sunlight that illumined it.

I wished at that moment that Winifred could have stood next to me. I wished she could have looked on her sister and felt as I did. For in that moment, I didn't want to be like me anymore. I wanted a heart like Rosie's.

If someone speaks an angry word to me, misunderstands me, or treats me unfairly—if someone even looks at me funny, I can carry it with me for days. It grows like a sore on my tongue. The worst part is, somehow, the pain gives me pleasure. I believe Winifred would understand what I mean.

Rosie has had enough pain and heartache to occupy her every thought for the rest of her life. And yet her new heart is already so filled with God's magnificent, all-consuming love, that there is no room for anger, bitterness, or hatred.

I want to be like that.

Judy looked up from the note and smiled. "Rosie, these are wonderful words."

"Well then, dear," Rosie said brightly, handing her an envelope, "let's put those wonderful words right in here."

Judy glanced at the address and with amusement said to me, "What do you think, Bob? Can our post office handle this?"

Rosie had written: "Winifred Rossi, Lower Mundane."

"It might take them a couple of years," I joked, "but I think they know where she lives. Shall we mail it for you, Rosie?"

"That would be so nice," she replied, hoisting herself out of her chair. "And here." She handed me Winnie's old letter. "Tuck this in there too."

Rosie motioned for us to follow her into the kitchen. "I wonder if you could help me with something else?"

She opened a drawer by the sink and removed an old candle. "Let's drip a little red wax on that," she said with a sparkle in her eye. "Might as well do it right. My sister hasn't received a letter from Rosie for a long time."

CHAPTER TWENTY-ONE

Grieving for Gilda

"I still can't believe it. I just can't believe she's gone forever."

Horace Dahlgren stood so still, his head slung between his sloping shoulders, his fists shoved deep into his pockets, his eyes staring at the spot in the parking lot where destiny had spoken its verdict and taken away his beloved Gilda.

"It seems like only yesterday I held her in my arms," he said, shaking his head. "We shared some beautiful years. And now... well, I just can't believe she's gone."

I had lived long enough to know there are times when it's best to just be with a friend in pain and keep your thoughts to yourself. But actually I was quite sure this was not one of those times.

I stood now beside my grieving buddy, unable to look him in the eye. I was unable to speak a word, not because I thought silence was more appropriate, but because I knew, if I even attempted a sound, I would laugh. And I wouldn't be able to disguise this one as a cough or a comforting chuckle. No this would be a full-fledged, phlegm-flinging guffaw. I might even have to lie on the ground.

"Gilda was the only one I ever wanted," he continued,

his voice breaking apart, which only made it worse for me. "I just can't believe it. I just cannot believe I backed over my own guitar with a school bus!"

"I'm sorry," I barely managed. "Did you wreck it?"

He looked at me bewildered and asked, "Do you mean did I wreck the bus or the guitar?"

That was all I could take. The sound that burst past my lips was explosive and sprayed my buddy badly. All he could do was stare at me in disbelief.

The accident happened this way. Horace is the youth pastor at Grace Megatabernacle, the only church in town large enough to have a full-time youth person. Friday night he drove a school bus of teens to Camp Whispering Meadows for the weekend. Upon returning Sunday afternoon, he let the kids off in the church parking lot and then decided he would sweep out the bus and drive it down the road to the Amoco for a wash. So he took his guitar, Gilda, a vintage rosewood Guild, out the back emergency door and put it on the ground while he swept. That's where he forgot about it until he returned with his dripping vehicle and discovered a pile of crushed case, splintered wood, flecks of mother of pearl, and twisted metal strings.

She *had* been a beautiful guitar, and I shouldn't have laughed. It was just one of those moments that struck me funny, made worse because laughter was an inappropriate response. It was like laughing in the choir loft during the Christmas cantata. The simple fact that it's forbidden makes everything funnier. But I knew I wouldn't be laughing if it had happened to me.

Musicians who play other instruments, particularly larger instruments, probably don't understand what it's like to "lose" a favorite guitar. Its small size is part of the instrument's appeal. It's so wonderfully portable that you tend to carry it with you. Over time you share a lot of experiences.

One of my buddies has collected stickers from everywhere he and his guitar have traveled. You wonder where he's played? Take about an hours and peruse his road case, a collage of pasted memories.

For twenty-five years now I've carried one guitar or another halfway around the world and back, and it never felt like the slightest bother. My guitar was usually part of the reason I was going places so I felt it belonged right there over my shoulder. I carried it the way a veteran photographer carries his favorite cameras or a tennis pro carries extra rackets. For each, the case is like an essential piece of clothing without which that person would feel only partially attired.

I'd slip the case's padded strap over my shoulder, shift my hips slightly, and the guitar would find its place balanced perfectly on my back. Often I'd forget it was even there.

"Oh no! I forgot my guitar on the plane."

"Oh, really, what's that over your shoulder?"

I don't think many other musicians have the same affection for their instruments. I think, for example, that it's different for those who play piano. They may "love" the special baby grand in the living room, but it's probably not the same one they practiced on so many hours at the conservatory. It's probably not the one they played at the competition, or first recorded on in the studio. And only the largest pianists ever try to heave one over their shoulder (usually these men and women have really fat hands and don't play well anyway). No, pianos don't fit in overhead racks or slide between the baby carriage and the diaper bag. Pianos stay where you put them, so they miss a lot.

Few other instruments are as sensually caressed as the guitar. The sound of an acoustic open chord not only shoots from the sound hole toward the listener but also resonates back through the guitar and right into the chest cavity like a sweet breath of music. Only the most avant garde pianists have experienced such closeness with their instrument.

Lower Mundane's very own Louis Donde Vondo might be the exception. Born Larry Donley, Louis never impressed his hometown much.

Even his old piano teacher Virginia Rykerd said "The boy had a need to perform, but he wasn't willing to put in the hours of practice necessary to become an accomplished pianist. Oh sure, he had some talent but absolutely no discipline. I tell you, if he hadn't been so implausibly weird, no one would have given him the time of day."

But Louis had his moment of fame. Between March and June of 1968 he performed his "Birth of a Pianist" in some museums of contemporary art. The work consisted of three movements, the first in which Donde Vondo, a small man, played from within the darkness beneath the lid of the piano. He may have been the first to do so. The second movement he played with his fingers on the keys, his arms protruding from beneath the lid. The third movement he sat in the buff but for a piece of strategically placed sheet music, playing melodies reminiscent of simple nursery rhymes.

Tens of people across the country proclaimed his work a modern masterpiece, but the New York Times said,

"'Birth of a Pianist' is a sad excuse for art, and Donde Vondo should get a real job."

Shortly thereafter a penniless Larry Donley returned to Lower Mundane and took the Times' advice. Last month he received his twenty-year pin at the tannery in Chastain. No one who he works with has ever heard of Louis Donde Vondo.

No, most pianists would not understand the closeness a guitarist feels toward his instrument. I think perhaps some cellists understand. I've watched a few buy an extra seat on the airplane so their "friend" can travel with them. Air travel costing what it does, that's an indication of true affection.

Cellists play sitting down, head bent low, arms and legs cradling their instrument, like a parent cuddling a chubby child. Perhaps they understand, but even so their instrument is not as accessible to the common person as the guitar.

The first guitar I remember was my Grandpa's. He called it a Hawaiian though most would recognize it today as a National Steel. He bought it out of the Sears and Roebuck catalogue for $33. Today, sixty years later, it hangs safely in my closet, probably worth thirty times what he paid for it.

Grandpa tried to show me how to play it like he did, laying the guitar flat on his lap, sliding a metal bar up and down the neck with his left hand, and plucking the strings with his right. I never got the hang of it. I wanted to hold it closer in my arms.

I still return to it several times each year, thinking I might grow to love it as Grandpa did. But age has caused a slight warp in the neck that makes the strings difficult to press, so I always tuck it back away.

The guitar has been in my possession since Grandpa died when I was fifteen, but it's never really been mine. If it could speak, the stories it would tell would be of its old friend, Albin. And that is as it should be.

Other guitars would speak of me. And I believe three in particular would speak of me fondly.

The Yairri Gakki: I was a college sophomore in Chicago riding the elevated train from the North Shore into the Loop. In my pocket I held tightly in my sweaty hand $240 in small bills. This is proof that the word 'sophomore' means 'wise fool.' I got off at Wabash, entered a building, and took an elevator up to the second floor. When the doors opened, I was in The Guitar Gallery where, hanging from the ceilings and every inch of available wall space, I saw hundreds of beautiful instruments. It took me all afternoon to play just those in my price range. I bought the Japanese classical.

It was with me for fifteen years. I wrote my first songs to my wife and then to my children with this lovely guitar. I recorded my first record albums with it. (Remember twelve-inch vinyl discs? We used to use what we called record players.) I sang in town halls, libraries, coffee houses, elementary schools, and churches as well as around campfires from my hometown in Pennsylvania to the heart of Africa. That guitar was my constant companion.

Several years ago when we moved our family from New England to the Midwest, I asked my closest friend if he would like to keep it. It has become for him a prized possession, and this makes me very happy.

The Martin 0021: This was a vintage antique built in 1928, the most finely constructed guitar I have owned. I only kept it for a few years because it was a tiny, fragile thing, which others had cared for so well and which I was slowly ruining. It was what they call a parlor guitar and not meant to withstand the rigors of the road. The only thing I hated worse than selling it was watching it destroyed, so sadly I let it go.

The Yamaha APX-20: This is the first new guitar I had bought in twenty years, and it was the only one I splurged on, buying the mother of pearl inlay around the body. The decoration does nothing to enhance the sound, but the guitar is gorgeous, and it sounds as good as it looks. It's an acoustic-electric so it doesn't sound great unless you plug it in, but oh, how it sounds when you do! I've had it for three years now, and it may be the last one I'll buy.

Three very different guitars. One nylon stringed, two steel. Two acoustic, one electric. One antique, two new. One fancy, two plain. But all have the characteristics of a fine instrument.

They all "want" to be in tune.

They all have great action.

They all resonate a beautiful sound.

There's nothing more frustrating than trying to tune a poor guitar. To be tuned, each string must endure a precise amount of tension, and the instrument a lot of stress. Too little tension on a string, and its pitch is flat. Too much and it's sharp. If any part of the instrument can't take the stress, then it can't be tuned.

I once stood tuning my guitar for twenty minutes before a couple of hundred people and three idle video cameramen drawing union pay. This is not the mark of a fine instrument or a fine performance. Fine instruments almost tune themselves. It's as if each string "knows" when enough is enough, finds its own pitch, and stays there. When you strum a chord, a flat string identifies itself as if asking to be tightened. It "wants" to be in tune.

A friend of mine, who is into new technology in music, enthusiastically predicts that soon there will be a perfect guitar that never needs to be tuned.

"It'll be awesome," he says. "You'll never have to replace another old string. Flip a switch, and it's perfectly tuned."

"Then it's not a guitar," I insist, "and I'd never buy it."

You see, guitars are imperfect. Tuning is part of the beauty of the instrument. And the ability to be tuned and to stay tuned is what separates the fine from the mediocre.

Once the guitar is tuned, comes the next test. How's the action? In other words, is it a joy to play?

I bought my first guitar as a young teenager. It was brand new, cost me $14.50, and as they say, "You get what you pay for." The action (the distance between the strings and the neck) was so high that it was nearly unplayable. My fingers bled. Even the best guitarists would have been unable to play it well.

Fine guitars, on the other hand, have quick, responsive action. You barely touch the string, and it's against the neck. You don't have to squeeze the string into submission; it's ready to bend at the slightest encouragement. This is the second mark of a fine instrument.

But there's one more test, and it's probably the most important. What does the guitar sound like? Now we're talking about craftsmanship and materials, design and construction.

If the wood is too heavy or overly braced, it won't resonate with the vibration of the string, and the sound will be dull. Or if it's constructed poorly, bracing will loosen, and it will develop rattles and buzzes. But when the woods are carefully chosen, crafted according to a good design, and constructed by skilled, loving hands, the result is an instrument that resonates deeply on the low end, brightly on the high end, and sustains the tone for a long time.

So if you have a guitar that won't stay in tune, is hard to play, sounds dull or rattles, you have one of two problems. You either have a poor instrument, or you have a fine one that's been damaged. If the latter is true, don't try to fix it yourself. Rather send it back to the one who made it. In the hands of the maker, it can always be redeemed. That is, unless it's been run over by a school bus. If that's happened, you can either throw it away or, like my friend, you can hang it on the wall of your garage.

"Would you like to see her?" Horace said, starting to chuckle a little himself.

"Oh," I said, wiping tears of laughter from my eyes, "I'm not sure I could take that."

"Ah, come on. Take a look."

It wasn't until we stood in his garage staring at the absurdly abstract sculpture of rosewood, spruce, and steel that something changed in my spirit. Suddenly, surprisingly, I felt sad.

Horace was starting to see some humor in his actions now. In fact, he looked as though he might crack up any minute, but just felt sad. As we stood in the garage among the old tires, cartop carriers, and cans of paint, it became for me a funeral parlor. A viewing. A visitation.

"Okay," I said soberly, holding my hands before me in surrender. "I know you're probably going to think I'm nuts, but at this moment a prayer comes to mind."

Now it was his turn to lose it.

"No, no," I protested, "I'm serious. You've heard it a thousand times. 'Make me an instrument, oh Lord.'"

"Yes, Lord," he muttered, "just don't let me end up like this guitar." And then we both laughed.

There was more to the prayer, but I didn't get to pray it that day. In fact, I didn't know the whole prayer then, but if I had it would have been something like this.

Oh, Lord, you have created me as a fine instrument, and not just any instrument. Lord, You have made me like a guitar. Therefore I am imperfect and in need of your care. Please always hold me close in your arms and help me to display the marks of your excellence.

Help me to desire to be spiritually in tune.

Help me to respond to your slightest touch.

Help my life to be like joyful music in your ears, resonating through my soul and back into you heart like a sweet breath of praise.

Oh, Lord, when I am damaged by the rigors of this world, help me to know that you can make me like new, even when I am splintered and broken.

And, God, when my earthly journeys are through, may all my stories be of you.

Amen.

When I left Horace that day I said, "Hey, I really am sorry about Gilda. She was a beauty."

"Thanks," he said. "I knew you'd understand."

CHAPTER TWENTY-TWO

The Easter Pageant at the Megatab

Just east of town on Route 6, half a mile this side of Tooters Bar and Grill, sprawls the beautiful Grace Megatabernacle, a "Nondenominational, Bible-believing, Spirit-filled, friendly family of faithful believers."

"It must be true." I overheard someone grumbling. "It's written in two-foot letters right across their big marquee."

The sarcasm is common. Most folks around here don't care much for the place.

It was born in 1980 from the discontent of two families, the Camerons and Speeners, who left our church, the Old White Church, to begin what they believed to be the only valid ministry in the area. Both families had been part of the Old White Church for less than a year when they had had enough. From their perspective the church was resistant to the Spirit of God.

Ultimately they founded Grace Megatabernacle. You can read the whole story in the eighty-page booklet entitled, "Great Is Thy Faithfulness: The Grace Megatabernacle Story."

Though the booklet tells of two families following God's leading, others in town interpret the events differently. I didn't have to read a thing to tell you that Cameron and Speener weren't from around here. Small towns are resistant to change even when initiated from within. If you are a transplant, you had better not try to change a thing, at least not very soon, or you'll hear your name mumbled in dark tones from some distant aisle in the grocery store. I learned this through personal experience.

During our first summer here, I could tell people weren't warming up to me. Pete Mundy finally gave in and told me it was because I'd hired a chemical company to spray my new lawn. I wondered aloud if it were an ecological concern.

"Oh no," Pete told me. "It's just that no one around here's ever hired a lawn company. Folks are kind of wonderin' who you think you are being the first." This is the way it is.

The Camerons and the Speeners moved here from Ohio, apparently on purpose, so right off people were raising their eyebrows quite high. The two families joined the church the first week and within a month began to submit proposals for the construction of additional parking lots, a new nursery, an external, forty-foot illuminated cross, and of all things, a multipurpose gymnasium-fellowship hall.

This is a church that hasn't seen more than fifty people on a Sunday morning since the great revival.

Even though these two new families swelled the membership to forty-seven, they understandably became an unwelcome irritant.

In fairness to Cameron and Speener, the Old White Church had for years exuded an exuberance bordering on comatose and probably did need a shot of spiritual adrenaline. In fairness to the church, when you've been nearly dead for so long you can't handle a lot of excitement. Parking lots and gymnasiums were just too much to consider. Acquisitions as small as a new plastic wastebasket or cork bulletin board routinely occupied the trustees for weeks.

Cameron and Speener's last proposal was for new pew pencils. As evidence for this need, they cited that the old ones were chewed and unpleasant to use. Speener offered to buy the pencils himself and place them in the pew registries. When the elders began to debate the appropriateness of the donation, the camel's back cracked loudly, and the two men walked out of the vestibule doors for the last time.

The rest of the story is in "Great Is Thy Faithfulness"—how the families worshiped the next Sunday in one of their basements, how they rented the elementary school gym for two years, how they named themselves Grace Megatabernacle when there were only fifteen members, how ten families invested a thousand dollars each and dedicated it to the Lord, how the land was donated, how the gymnasium, parking lot, and illuminated cross were paid for with cash. It's all there. The booklets are free in the narthex. You can make a small donation toward the expense of publishing them if you wish.

What you won't read about in the booklet is the personality clash and power struggle between the Megatab's founders and their new pastor, the Reverend Harold Coates. What you won't learn either is that the Camerons and the Speeners left the church three years ago and are said to be somewhere in California. It's rumored they're no longer even involved with a congregation. No one at the Old White Church is surprised, and lamentably no one seems very sad about it either. The Megatab, however, continues to prosper.

Few folks in Lower Mundane attend there, but about 1500 drive out from the city every Sunday morning. My family and I joined them not long ago.

Though words like *upbeat, theatrical,* and yes, *charismatic* could all be used to describe the worship service, perhaps the word *pageantry* says it best. Choirs sing from the balcony. Dancers flit up the side aisles. The orchestra, rising on hydraulics, seemingly appears from nowhere. Dramatic lighting directs your every eye movement. All the services are productions, but of course none are more spectacular than those staged at Christmas and Easter.

Last Christmas, in an attempt to top the year before, the cast swelled to 120, including the baby Jesus, who was only four days old (people had prayed for months about that one). Twenty angels hovered overhead on nearly invisible wires and then flew away into the balcony on their way to Bethlehem. Long gossamer robes trailed like the wind behind them. Forty real animals were involved, including a camel imported from a farm in Indiana, and a dozen realistic creature mannequins of mostly the mule and cow varieties were also utilized. The production was performed flawlessly for eight sell-out crowds, and no one was disappointed.

Then came Easter.

We were fortunate to get tickets for the one performance people will be talking about for a long time, the one that will surely never be repeated. UPI carried a story about it, as did *USA Today*, a number of local news stations, and even "Entertainment Tonight."

Once again angels adorned the ceiling. Once again animals bleated and mooed along with the church choir and orchestra, each beefed up with professionals from the city. The auditorium was transformed majestically from Jerusalem, to Gethsemane, to Golgotha, to the tomb, and to the upper room.

It was splendid, and it would have been perfect had Jesus not fallen off the cross. To say the least, it took us all by surprise.

Since the actor wore no upper garment, it was impossible to use a harness to hold him during the crucifixion scene. Instead the prop committee designed something like a retractable bicycle seat that the actor could straddle. Leather thongs then held his arms to the cross. As one of the stagehands later explained on Channel 3, "The mechanism had never failed before."

We couldn't see exactly what happened, but apparently the seat gave way. When only one leather thong broke, the actor came swinging down sideways, still attached by one hand. Twisting uncontrollably, he kicked the head off a mannequin cow. The head slid the entire length of the stage, finally stopping at the feet of a horrified Roman soldier.

There it spun slowly to a stop like a hairy hubcap. The solder, trying desperately to stay in character, casually kicked it offstage, as if dealing with cow pieces was a routine part of a centurion's duties. All the while Jesus spun helplessly by one arm, the thong tightening painfully on his wrist, his feet inches above the ground. No one came to help.

After perhaps thirty seconds the lights went out, and we watched penlights running from backstage toward the cross. I heard the conductor whispering hoarsely into his headset, "We can't play the overture. We can't see a thing down here!" I heard the panicked voice of a stage manager complaining that the cross was jammed and couldn't be lowered, followed by, "Just get him down! Get him down!"

Then we *all* heard Jesus, shouting in an agonized but commanding voice, "No, get me back up there now!"

Our vision having adjusted to the darkness, we watched Jesus crawl onto the shoulders of several actors and a stagehand. Then the orchestra began to play softly. The lights eased up, and the play continued with Jesus straddling the seat, still tied tightly by one hand and clinging to the cross with the other. The rest of the cow had been removed.

Surprisingly I only felt a tinge of embarrassment and amusement. Somehow, to me, what happened seemed okay. On the way out I spoke to several people in the lobby. With the exception of one woman who commented, "Oh, I feel so bad about what happened to Jesus," everyone else thought the performance was beautiful and moving despite the interruption. Of course, that's not the way the media presented it.

In our information age, a story like this travels fast, so within a day, articles began to appear in newspapers across the country. They were mostly short articles, humorous human-interest stuff. The United Press headline read "Jesus Falls Off Cross," while several trashier tabloids used leads like "Messiah Kills Milk Cow." My mother told me that in Buffalo, an anchorman closed a broadcast with, "And where else could it happen, folks, but in a town called Lower Mundane?"

People around here took it fairly well. After all, we're not apt to hear about our town on "Good Morning, America" for a very long time. We may as well enjoy it. Most of the articles made their way on to the bulletin board at Henny's Barber shop, and even the Megatab put up a couple in their visitation center. After a few weeks things quieted down.

However, something felt wrong to me. It was the same nagging feeling when someone interrupts my thoughts, and I can't remember what it was that was bothering me. I try to remember what the problem was so I can worry about it, but then I worry even more because I can't remember what it was I was supposed to be worrying about. Well, the feeling was something like that.

About a month later, in a bus at the airport, I met the actor who played Jesus. I learned that he is presently studying at the university for a master's degree but drives a parking shuttle part-time on weekends. I complimented him on his fine performance even with the mishap. We visited a while, and he showed me his wrist, still badly sprained and bandaged tightly six weeks after the performance.

"It hurt like crazy," he told me, laughing. "But hey, I had to go back up on the cross, or we'd have some serious theological problems. Right? No crucifixion, no resurrection.

Or as my grandma says, "If you don't grind the beans, you can't drink the coffee.'"

At that moment I understood why I had felt bothered. Not surprisingly all those humorous stories had missed the point. Not one mentioned the guy's wrist. Not one mentioned that he could have quit. But instead, when the stagehands and centurions tried to take him off the cross, he took charge and said, "No, get me back up there *now!*"

Not one of the news reporters quipped, "What do you suppose Jesus would have done had *he* fallen off the cross?"

If they had dared to wonder that, they might have seen the truth. Jesus would have done the same. For it was *his* intent to be on that cross. It was *his* plan all along. No one could have taken him off. Pilate thought *he* put Jesus up there. The mob thought *they* were vindicated, but Jesus was in control the whole time, right where he had planned to be. The young man's grandma was right. No ground beans, no rich coffee. No Place of the Skull, no right hand of God. No Good Friday, no Easter morning.

I don't know why the Camerons and Speeners left town. Perhaps they had good reason. I also don't know where they are, but I'm sure they've heard about the faux pas at the Megatab. They could hardly have missed it. Jay Leno read the headlines for a week. I would like them to know though that the production was not just the joke everyone made it out to be. I would like them to know how moving and provocative it was. In one way, it may have been the most magnificent Easter pageant ever.

CHAPTER TWENTY-THREE

One More Uniform

For it is by grace you have been saved,
through faith—and this not from yourselves,
it is the gift of God—not by works,
so that no one can boast.

(Ephesians 2:8-9)

This was a high day in Lower Mundane. Certainly it was higher than Ground Hog Day or Washington's Birthday. Probably it was a little lower than Christmas but sadly, for some, right up there with Easter. This was the day that nearly every little boy (and many little girls) between the ages of six and ten gathered after school to sign up for Little League baseball.

My pastor, Ryan Care, is coaching for his third season, and once again he's fired up. I saw him at the post office this morning. Ryan's always a cheerful guy, but this drizzling, April morning his excitement was splashing all over.

"What a great day!" he nearly cheered, smiling bigger than ever. "I love it! I just *love it!*"

Here is a man whose church has grown far more slowly than he had hoped; attendance last week was eighteen. Here's a man who is almost always out of money. Our organist, who is also church chairman, just followed a job opportunity out of the area, and just last evening Ryan's daughter called home from college to say she had decided to go ahead and "missionary date" the Mormon kid. Why was this man so happy? Was it the joy of the Lord?

Well, yes. But it was also the first day of Little League in Lower Mundane. I wish I could be so enthusiastic, but baseball never did much for me. Indeed, I really only have one pleasant memory of the game. But it is a tenacious one.

"Okay, boys, when I call your name, please indicate your presence by saying 'here.'"

Mr. Love still wore his suit pants, white shirt, and tie from our classroom, but he had replaced his sports coat with a heavy gray, hooded sweatshirt and instead of his shiny black, round-toed wing tips, he now sported a clean pair of white canvas high-topped tennies. Completing the outfit, on the top of his head sat a stiff new Pittsburg Pirates cap.

"Mark Engle," he barked.

"Here."

"Christopher Richardson."

"Here."

"Dale Spazkey."

"Present!"

Once again everyone laughed. Spaz always said "present" instead of "here," and everyone always laughed, including me, though I never got the joke.

One time I even tried it myself, but nobody laughed at *me*. Nobody even giggled.

However, once again, people were carrying on as if Spazkey were Jackie Gleason or J. Fred Muggs, which only added to my suspicion I didn't belong in this group. This concerned me a lot. You see, I wanted to be one of these guys. I really wanted to be a part of this team. A real Little Leaguer.

"Butch Sinsabaugh," Mr. Love continued.

"Here."

"Bobby Stromberg."

"Here," I shouted.

Quite honestly I didn't think there was much chance I'd be "here" for long. I was sure I wouldn't make the team. For the previous three or four years I'd played in the farm league with nearly every other boy in the primary grades, but you didn't have to *make* that team. You just showed up. That, of course, was good, but then again you didn't get uniforms or ride in buses or anything. You just showed up and chose sides and played against your buddies, so it wasn't like being on a real team.

"Larry Vandenhouk."

"Here."

"Timmy Wyman."

"Here."

"And Daniel Zook."

"Here."

"Okay, fellas, welcome to tryouts," Mr. Love said with a warm smile. He opened a cardboard box full of shiny, clean, white, rubber-coated baseballs. "Let's count off. Give me two lines. And let's throw each other some grounders."

I didn't like grounders. I mean, I didn't mind throwing them, but I didn't like trying to catch them because baseballs are too hard.

"Come on, boys, put that glove down in the dirt so the ball can't get past you. Come on now, keep an eye on the ball."

Fat chance! I'd learned long ago about keeping an eye on the ball and vice versa. If you shoved your glove in the dirt where it belonged, that ball would surely hop up at the last split second and pop you right in the face. On the other hand, if you lifted your glove off the ground to protect your face, the ball would hop lower. The impact then was potentially far more painful and embarrassing.

No, I'd found the best way to handle a hot grounder was to straighten my spine, throw my head back and over my shoulder, twist my body sideways, and blindly swipe at the ball. It looked a little like ballet. Occasionally the ball would actually stick in my glove, which was really stiff, nearly the length of my arm, and weighed about three pounds.

"Okay, boys, let's line up for some batting practice, and those of you who think you have the stuff to be a pitcher, head on out to the mound."

I hated batting practice. To my knowledge the batting "T" had not been invented in 1962. This meant hitting the ball was almost impossible.

Today kids have it easy, but even so I'm amazed children ever learn how to play the game well enough to enjoy it. I've watched kids swinging a bat twice their height at a ball sitting motionless on top of a "T" and still strike out. I've watched kids lose a bat too heavy to control and hit a five-year-old catcher right in the shins. I've watched a kid, with his helmet falling over his face, try to find first base, and run right into the backstop. This is not a fun game to learn.

As I stood in the batting line, there was no "T" to put the ball on. I had to face a hyperactive kid who had had a bunch of hot dogs and chocolate milk for lunch and hadn't touched a baseball since last summer. The ball might fly into the dugout, or it might hit me right in my arching back. You never could tell. No, this was not a fun game to learn.

And it wasn't a particularly fun game to play either, mainly because of the parents. Ordinary parents, nice people like my doctor, the bank president, the school cook, the Jewell Tea man, and the Catholic priest (I think he was a parent—people called him "Father") all became homicidal at our ball games.

I know I will never forget the angry snarls and unintelligible curses when, as a first grader, my team was down by one run in the bottom of the last inning with two outs and one man on. That was the moment I hit a homer. With my eyes closed, I *hit a homer!* You would think this would be a time for celebration, but no. All because I inadvertently passed my teammate, who wouldn't leave third base. And the truth is, he would have gone all the way home if the parents hadn't been climbing the chicken-wire backstop, barking at him.

The outfielders were trying to get the ball out of the creek so there was plenty of time, but he saw those parents looking like rabid dogs at the pound, and he just froze. So I passed him. How was I to know?

"Okay, boys," Mr. Love yelled, scratching some notes on his clipboard. "Let's have all the number twos on defense. Richardson, catcher. Danny, first base. Timmy, second base. Doug, short. Butch, third…"

I didn't even bother to listen for my name. I just picked up my glove and headed out toward right field. Right field where the ball never flies. Right field where the bees swarm in the clover. Right field where they don't even bother mowing the grass. Right field, the un-position.

No, I really never cared for this game of baseball. The ball was too hard. The bat too heavy. My glove too big. The innings too long. The summer too hot. The parents too canine.

So why did I spend a couple of hours every day after school for two weeks trying to make a team that played a game I wasn't any good at and didn't even like? Because I wanted to be included. I wanted to be one of the guys.

Every summer I'd eat my Wheaties early in the morning with my dad. I'd feel the smooth, sweat-stained, leather band of my wool baseball cap against my forehead. I'd smell my leather glove intermingled with my dad's Old Spice as, peering close together out our picture window through a cool blanket of gray fog, my dad would say softly, "Oh, boy, Bobby, when this burns off, it's going to be another scorcher."

Then, out of swirling gray, we would see my gang of buddies materialize like ghosts, pumping hard, standing on rubber pedals, arms bent, heads low to the handlebars, and braking fast with blasts of sand in our dirt driveway.

"Hey, Strommy, you ready?"

With a hug, I'd shoot out the door, thread my glove over my handlebars, and off my friends and I would go. Together.

For all my summers we had done this baseball stuff *together*. Now I didn't know what would happen, because for us to stay together, I had to make *this* team, and I probably wouldn't.

There were only eighteen uniforms. Twenty-seven of us had signed up to play. Three had dropped out the first week. Six of us would be cut.

Going into the second week, it became clearer who those six would be—five others and me. Of those other five, none of them were my close buddies. So I desperately gave it everything I had. In grounder drills I kept my glove in the dirt, even after taking a few bad hops.

In the outfield I stayed alert with my hands on my knees, chattering at my pitcher louder than all the others, "Hum, Babe, hum, Babe, attaboy, attaboy!" If there had been bees, I would have ignored them.

In batting practice, when I struck out, every time I went down swinging.

I never walked anywhere. From the outfield to the bench, from the bench to the plate, and back to the bench, I always trotted. If I had hit the ball, even a little dribble to the pitcher, I would have run my hardest.

But at the end of the two weeks I realized my best wasn't going to be enough.

"Boys, I know this will be hard for some of you," Mr. Love said, "and I want you to know how much I appreciate every one of you and your good effort. But," he raised his eyebrows with a pained expression, "unfortunately we only have eighteen uniforms. I want you to know that if you don't make the team today, I am going to need at least one extra boy to be team manager."

"Oh! Oh! Please! Please! Can I, please?" Jimmy Dougherty, an older boy who had tried out for the last three years and never made the team, jumped up and down, waving his arm in his own uniquely awkward way.

"Well, Jim," Mr. Love said kindly, "thank you. I think it would be great if you'd like to help me again this summer."

And then almost looking my way, he added, "The rest of you, of course, need to know that you are all welcome to come and watch any of our practices. And we'd love to have you cheering us on during the season."

This was no consolation to me.

"Now, here are the boys who made the team for this summer. Butch Sinsabaugh, Larry Vandenhouk, Dale Spazkey…"

Two of the rejects, wisely, hadn't bothered to come that day. Two others were twin brothers who didn't seem to care. Of course, Jimmy Dougherty was thrilled and acted as if he had pulled a coup, but I was crushed.

In a celebration parade of hoots, howls, and Tarzan calls, the "chosen" followed Mr. Love into the parking lot. There, from the trunk of his blue Fairlane, they each received a brown paper shopping bag containing a clean new uniform.

"Awright, I got number 6!"

"Who got 16? Hey, Spaz, you want to trade?"

Then they were out of the parking lot, off and flying, pedaling fast… as team. We had ridden to practice together, but now I hung back by the bike rack until they were out of sight.

Mr. Love was over on the field putting the bats in a large canvas bag and tossing the balls into a wire milk-bottle basket.

"See you later, Mr. Love," I yelled, trying not to show too much disappointment.

"See you in class, Strommy," he shouted cheerily, swinging the heavy bag over his shoulder. Then struggling to hoist the basket onto his hip he added, "Say, Bobby, how about a hand here?"

Running back, I grabbed the basket with both hands and pulled it up onto the front of my leg. In silence we walked together back to his car.

"You can put those right in there beside the spare tire," he said, pointing in the trunk.

Then my breath caught in my throat. There in his trunk was one more brown paper shopping bag.

No, it couldn't be, I thought, hoping against hope. *It's probably some old clothes to take to the cleaners, or canned goods, or a carton of grape Nehi. It couldn't be another uniform.*

Mr. Love was squeezing the bats in between the spare tire and the shopping bag, unaware that my heart was racing.

"Mr. Love," I asked, surprised to hear the words coming out of my mouth, "whatcha got there in the shoppin' bag?"

"Oh," he said with a chuckle, "that's just an old..."

Suddenly understanding the true meaning of my question, he stopped in mid-sentence and began to stammer, uncertain how to answer. Then he decided to tell me the truth. "Why, Bobby, that's just… why it's a…well… actually it's an old uniform from a couple of years ago. I must have pulled it out of the closet by mistake."

Opening up the bag, he pulled out a jersey shirt. Number four. It was made of a much heavier wool than the new uniforms, but it was the same light gray with the same soft blue pinstripes. Reaching into the bag, pretending to scowl, he pulled out the pants, which displayed a good sized rip in the knee. I could see in the bottom of the bag that the high socks were badly faded.

"Gee, it looks pretty good to me," I said, now afraid to look at Mr. Love, my heart pounding through my chest.

There was a long pause as, embarrassed, I stared into the trunk. I don't think Mr. Love knew what to say.

Then once again composed, confident, jovial, he spoke. "You know, by golly, I think that old uniform is just about your size, Bobby. You think you would mind wearing that old thing?"

"Really?" I said, feeling tears in my eyes.

"Of course you'd probably have to have your mom sew that knee up," he said, laughing. "I don't think it would survive another slide into home plate." Then he bundled the uniform into the bag and put it in my arms. "See you Monday, Bobby."

Ten minutes later I slid my bike into our driveway and, holding the old brown paper bag over my head, screamed, "Mom! Dad! I'm on the team! I made it!"

Of course I knew I didn't deserve to be on the team. I knew I hadn't earned my spot. I knew my best was not nearly good enough. But with grace, it doesn't matter.

CHAPTER TWENTY-FOUR

Why I Live Here

Thus far I've not written in these pages about my vocation. However, I wouldn't want to leave the impression that I am independently wealthy, that I spend my weeks building my new home and then running off to the airport to fly about the country. This would not be quite true.

Instead, for twenty years now I've had the same unusual job. Nearly every Friday and sometimes on Thursday, I say good-bye to my family and drive to the airport where I park my car, check in my luggage, and get on a plane. The plane then flies me to some other town. Usually the town is in the U.S. or Canada but not always. Occasionally it's in the Bahamas, Mexico, or some place in Europe.

Once there, I am greeted at the airport by a person I've never met. While waiting for my luggage, we talk to each other and smile as if we are good friends. Then we get into a car, and I am driven to an auditorium. Sometimes a hundred people are waiting. Sometimes several thousand. The size has never mattered much to me.

Soon somebody introduces me to the crowd, and I begin to talk or sing. For the next hour and a half they listen to me. Often when I'm telling them about myself, they laugh loudly. Often when I'm telling them about God, they become very quiet and lean forward in their seats.

When I'm done, people clap appreciatively, and the person who picked me up at the airport says something like "That was magnificent, just magnificent!" He hands me a check and drops me off at a hotel.

The next morning I'm taken back to the airport, where I board another plane and fly somewhere else to do the same thing again. At the end of the weekend I fly back home, pick up my car, and return excitedly to my family.

In some ways the actual job is quite easy for me. What's difficult is the process of getting there and the process of being invited in the first place. That's why it's so important that many people say, "That was magnificent, just magnificent!" If they mean it, then they will almost certainly tell someone else, and others will call and ask if I can do the same thing for them. That's how I've stayed busy all these years.

I always try hard to do the best job I can, but sometimes I fail to meet my own expectations. Fortunately, even so, people say words like "Magnificent," and I don't discourage them. It's very important in this work that people perceive me to be at least better than I really am.

I could hire a manger to tell people that I'm magnificent. He or she could make sure that articles about me were published and pictures of me appeared regularly in prominent publications. This heightened visibility would impress readers, who would then hire me before they would hire someone else. The public's elevated perceptions translate directly into increased dollars.

There are some advantages to this approach, the most obvious being that even when I'm not magnificent my manager could tell people that I am; that way I could keep busy even if I shouldn't be.

There is a downside to this arrangement, however. These professional prevaricators don't work cheaply, and they're often insistent that the beneficiary of their embellishment lives in a magnificent place like New York or L.A. These particular locales help to create illusions of magnificence.

I've never hired a manager because I've noticed a dangerous tendency in people like myself to believe the promotion they pay for. Intuitively I've sensed that as soon as I allow that to happen, that is to say, as soon as I begin to believe that I am indeed great, then the end will be near. At least all ministry will cease at that point.

Recently, following a particularly good performance for an unusually wonderful audience, a young man asked me how I control my ego, how I keep from getting a big head. I told him, "It's easy. I live in Lower Mundane."

This town is intolerant of illusions. People around here are not at all impressed with me. They not only refuse to believe all the great things that others around the country are saying, but they also refuse to even accept me as one who is worthy to belong here. Because I am not native to this area, meaning I wasn't born locally, I'll always be an alien, a nobody.

Walk into the Old Corner Store acting like you're someone special and see how long it takes to buy a pack of gum. You might have to wait all morning. That's the way it is in this town, and there is something right about it.

I've discovered a wonderful thing here. If you want to be seen as magnificent in Lower Mundane, then you serve other people, and you don't talk about it. Then you will slowly notice a warm openness where once there was only cold distrust. But even then you are not applauded, not ever. You are just loved.

This serving others does not come easily to me. It is not my natural inclination. Through my profession I've become accustomed to adulation and praise. I find very little of either in serving others. It takes too much time, often goes unnoticed, and is not particularly pleasant work. There is a strong part of me that would much rather serve myself. Fortunately, though, I've learned that serving *me* does not ultimately satisfy anyone.

God has called me to serve *others*. Ironically, in my work, this attitude of service only brings me more adulation. But adulation is temporal. It is here today and gone today too. It is not a source of sustaining joy. True joy comes in simply being obedient to God and serving as he directs. In my life, God's call to service goes far beyond vocation.

He has called me to serve as a husband to Judy and a father to Nate and Lars. He has called *us*, aliens in this world, to serve in this town. At times it seems a thankless task. But then God sends helpers like Ryan and Janine Care. God sends challenges like George Tudor and Rosie Serillo. We see lives changed, and we are blessed with joy.

When I leave this earth, I do not desire or expect to hear God say, "That was magnificent, just magnificent!" If he does, I imagine there will be a long pause, perhaps the equivalent of a millennium or two. During this time he'll allow the absurdity of the statement to saturate the "moment." He'll be very patient, because his comedic timing is impeccable, and because he knows I'm not real quick. Then finally I'll realize God has been pulling my leg as only he can, and we'll both crack up. The weatherman on Channel 5 will probably report hearing some thunder on the northern horizon.

I can imagine God wiping tears of laughter from his eyes, each droplet birthing a new galaxy or two. I can imagine him holding his magnificent hands out to me. The same hands that made the heavens and the earth, ice storms, earthworms, northern pike, mice, geese, baby's breath, music, color, Beethoven, and Van Gogh.

I can imagine my shame as I say to him, "Oh, Lord, you know that the only magnificence that has touched this mundane man has been from you."

Then I pray he will utter what I long to hear him say. It won't be "You sure were a great performer! Remember that night in Pittsburgh?" It won't be "Boy, you sure sold a bunchitude of those little books and videotapes, didn't ya?"

No, even on earth those things would fail to give me sustaining joy, and they will fail to give me saving grace in eternity.

I pray that I will hear him say, "Well done, my good and faithful *servant*."

This weekend I'll drive to the airport again, and I'll fly off to another town to do my work. I'm not going because some manager got me a job. I'm going because God has provided an opportunity to serve. When I'm finished, I'll fly back home, because God has called me to serve here too. That's what makes Lower Mundane "home to some of the world's people," a magnificent place to live. God meets me here. May it be so where you are as well.

AGMV Marquis

MEMBRE DE SCABRINI MEDIA

Québec, Canada
2004

Printed in Canada